MY PRETTY DOLL

The Halloween Special

LoveBite Shorts

ISBN: 9798857138755
Imprint: Independently published

Cover design by: Art Painter
Library of Congress Control Number: 2018675309
Printed in the United States of America

CONTENTS

FOREWARNING

This book is over-the-top craziness. If anything offends you, profanity, darkness (non-everything), lack of morals, cruelty, breeding, stalking, captivity, name-calling, objectification, golden showers (dear God, so much of it). Please return this book and never look here again. Ever. No seriously. Don't do it. Burn the image from your mind because Zak is not stable and never will be. This is my Halloween dark special. If you feel brave enough, read on but don't say I never warned you.

Good Luck!

With all my Love,

LoveBite Shorts xXx

PART I

CHAPTER 1

Zak

I gasped for breath as I sprinted over the driveway, flying over the featured water fountain to my front door. Ignoring the burn in my lungs, I check my watch and feel the satisfaction of knowing I have beat my previous record. With every success comes the debilitating knowledge that the only person I want to share my life with is no longer with me.

Any feeling of joy or pride dissipates. I take off on a gentle jog around my home to cool down. Ten minutes later, I walk to the memorial I have for my mother. She loved roses. She would take small cuttings from public parks and try to grow them in our mould-ridden council allocated shitty apartment. I planted every colour of the rose plant here in the hope that she would look over me when I came here each morning. Every day I ask for forgiveness here.

"I love you, Mum. I miss you every day. Rest easy."

She was a believer, so I live in the hope that her God is looking after her. The guilt never gets any easier. I stand up from the granite memorial plaque. I read over the words I repeat from within my soul every day.

> *Mum, you are the most precious memory I*
> *hold in my head, heart and soul.*

I stand up and stretch my back out before rotating my neck. My humanity was lost with my mother's life. I turn my back on her and switch back to cutthroat business mode.

* * *

I sip on my fourth coffee. My only reason to work is to keep my brain from entering dark and dangerous places. It took years of intensive therapy to stop myself from self-destructing.

I smirk when I think of the people whom I destroyed. Some are dead, and some live wishing they were dead.

The messenger pings on my laptop.

Benny: *This programme is killing me. Can you have a look at it when you get a chance?*

Me: *Sure. How are things with you today?*

I've known Benny for three years. He is an agoraphobic programmer. We are of a similar age. I don't know if it's because of his condition or personality, but he is the one human I can tolerate. My gut tells me it's because he hasn't been exposed and corrupted by society and has an almost innocent outlook on life.

Benny: *If I tell you something, will you promise not to judge me?*

I frown at the message box. I hope to fuck he isn't going to disappoint me.

Me: *Go ahead. You're in a safe message box.*

I'm damned curious as to what he has to say. The man eats, shits, works and sleeps. In the three years I've known him, he tried to go into his garden once and was a mess.

Benny: *You know my situation. I'm twenty-eight, and I can't meet girls in normal circumstances. I just wanted to do something different. To feel something different. I watched a documentary following a man who kept a silicone doll as his partner…*

I bend my neck to scan his message. I snort out laughter that rarely comes to me. Benny is going to fucking kill me one day with his antics.

What the fuck?

Me: *When are you getting married to her? Does she have any friends?*

Benny: *Fuck off, you cunt. You said this was a fucking safe message box!*

Me: *I'm messing with you. You know I hate most people and work from home to avoid the assholes that I employ.*

Benny: *I got one, and it's the best thing I ever did. You won't believe how lifelike these dolls are. Expensive but worth every penny.*

I cringe at the thought of fucking a plastic doll, but I understand why he needs this. My mother had taught me to treat all women with respect. Now? I do what I want.

I had given Jessica everything, but for her to go behind my back and fuck my best friend at the time was unforgivable. They are two fucks who are living in misery. One is a crack whore, and the other is in jail for a murder he didn't commit. All carefully conspired by yours truly.

Benny: *Hello? Fuck. I shouldn't have mentioned it.*

Me: *My mind wandered off. Look, you do you. I'm glad if it helps you cope and makes you happy.*

Benny tried to meet women with similar conditions, but it had been disastrous.

Benny: *The only reason I wanted to mention it is because I know you don't like women.*

I don't correct Benny. It's not that I don't like women. I find all people intolerable. My mind flicks to my mum. She was the only person I loved with all my heart, and knowing she died for me, no one will ever compare to the sacrifices she made for me.

Me: *Thanks for thinking about me and my dick.*

Benny: *You're an asshole. I don't know why we are still friends.*

Benny has a few other online friends. He doesn't know that I hacked into his entire 'secure' system to ensure he wasn't like the rest of them. He is my only friend, and I'm happy to keep it this way.

Me: *No, seriously, tell me more about her.*

Benny: *Fuck you. I'm going back to work.*

With a chuckle, I close the message box and return to work.

CHAPTER 2

Zak

I sip my champagne and hope the pain of being at a public event will alleviate some of my guilt. I rarely make any public appearances. Whenever I do, the media whore's dial up to a frenzy. I ignore the speculative looks and walk to my table, which is front and centre to the podium.

I sit at the side of the table to view the podium and the rest of the hall. The need to see any incoming assholes is essential.

My attention towards the speeches and presentations is minimal. I will be donating a substantial amount but not without making the homeless foundation sign a contract ensuring every penny is spent on the needy and not the executive assholes who run the charity.

"We will take a short break and serve dinner before we continue. Thank you for attending, and I hope you can see the importance of the work we strive to do."

I cover my mouth to prevent my yawn from showing as the last presenter wanders away from the podium.

"What do you mean my table isn't at the front? Do you know who I am?"

I close my eyes at the whining tone of a woman. It's good to know that everyone in attendance cares about the cause.

I smile at the waiter, who places my food before me. My mouth waters at the juicy looking steak. The amount I work out, I need constant calories. I try to shut out the whining bitch and enjoy my food.

After a few delicious bites, my peace is disturbed by the bitch who doesn't stop whining. My fingers tighten around my cutlery in anger. I swallow my food calmly before turning around to see the back of a woman arguing with someone who must be part of the event management.

"I am Lady Linden. Please address me correctly."

My anger vanishes as the amusement at her predicament takes precedence. My body relaxes against the seat, and I cut another portion of my steak to watch the show unfold before me.

My eyes rove the back of her body. She is wearing a red dress that clings to her ass, but her bare back is crisscrossed with tiny black straps.

The staff member is trying to pacify the spoilt bitch. She flicks her blond hair over her shoulder, causing her hair to cascade down her back, spoiling my view of her bare back.

"I want this addressed right this moment. I will not be moving until you move our table. This is an insult."

I can see the staff member straighten her back as she says something, but I'm not within hearing distance. Whatever it was, it didn't go down well with the Lady. She swings around, scanning the front row tables.

Her hair bounces around her face. I take in her pretty features. She is beautiful, with wide bright blue eyes, high cheekbones and thick, plump pink lips. She probably has them stuffed with filler. It's a tragedy that such beauty comes with a foul interior.

She spots me looking at her, and she points over at me.

"There, that man is sitting on his own. I demand that we be seated over there."

I tilt to the side and see two other young women beside her. The blonde woman is the ring leader. One woman looks embarrassed by the situation, and the other looks bored.

I carry on eating and draw my gaze away from them. There is no way in hell I will have any of those vapid bitches at my table. I purchased the entire table to avoid this situation.

CHAPTER 3

Elizabeth

I ignore the protesting woman and walk towards the man hogging an entire table to himself. The bastards should have put us at the front table. I'm reduced to making a scene at a shitty charity event. Everyone in the country knows who the Linden family is.

I compose myself and put my sultry look on. It never fails to convert men into dithering idiots.

"Excuse me, Sir. Could we join you at your table? There has been a terrible mix-up tonight with the tables."

I came here in place of my parents, and I will not lose an opportunity to look altruistic. The opportunity rarely occurs, and with a few carefully crafted pictures at this event, it might appear that I give a fuck about the homeless.

When the man looks up from his meal, my breath catches in my throat. He is damn handsome. His blue eyes are a shade darker than mine. Irrespective of the tux covering his upper body, he looks muscular and powerful.

I'm not too keen on his dark hair, however. I prefer the blonde Brad Pitt look alike. I frown at his jawline. Could he not have bothered to shave for the event?

When my eyes return to him, I notice him looking at my chest. I smirk. This will be easy. His eyes glanced up at me briefly before he focused on his food again.

I almost stomp my foot until I remember wearing my favourite Jimmy Choo's.

"Excuse me, Sir?" I said in a tight voice.

When he continues to chew his food and ignore me, I glare at the top of his head. How fucking rude?

I slap my clutch onto the table, and he continues to cut into his steak. I slap my other hand down on the table, leaning down to see his face.

"Are you fucking deaf?" I hissed at him.

His head finally lifts from his plate, and he pops a piece of meat into his mouth. My eyes flick down to his lips as he licks them.

He lifted his shoulder in a half shrug before lifting his red wine and raising it to his lips.

My eyes narrow in on his. He is ignoring me. Me! Lady Elizabeth Linden.

He places his glass on the table and delicately dabs his lips with a white napkin. Perhaps he could have passed for a gentleman if it wasn't for his poor manners and gorilla-shaped paws.

Why am I abasing myself in front of someone of little importance? I swing away from him, flicking my hair back and face my girls. They are looking at the man. I snap my fingers at them.

"Let's go sit down," I said stiffly, not wanting to say anything further in front of the odious man.

I march towards the table that the bitch had allocated for us. I'm going to ensure Daddy has her fired.

Once we sit down, it's not long till our food arrives. I grimace at the food my parents ordered.

"Don't you have a vegan option?" I asked the server. It's the latest trend.

"No. I'm sorry, Miss. We do have a vegetarian option. It's caramelised red onions and goat's cheese tartlets with a rocket salad."

I suppose I could eat the salad and the pastry crust. My pills suppress my appetite so that I won't need much.

I look at Cecelia and Marie, who are eating the food given to them. The bitches will probably throw it all up in the toilets later.

"Fine, it will need to do."

I will email the foundation regarding their shoddy menus. I watch my friends eat before I look around to see where the best spot is to take some pictures. Smiling when I see the perfect place, I pull out my mirror to check my hair and face. These fat heifers can make themselves useful after they have stuffed their faces.

I glance at Marie. She looks good tonight.

"Are you sure you should be eating that, Marie?" I said with faux concern.

She frowns slightly and puts her fork down from the beef.

"You're right." She waves the waiter over for some drinks.

I smirk into my mirror before snapping it shut.

"Yes, let's hope the drink is better than everything else I've had to endure here tonight."

Cecelia glances at me.

"Do you know who that was?"

I frown at her in confusion.

"The man you spoke to for the table." She said in an exasperated tone.

My eyes flick towards him. He looked at his phone.

"I don't recognise him," I said, looking back at Cecelia.

"That's because he isn't caught on camera much. That is Zak Henderson, the tech billionaire. Rumour has it he is fucked up in the head and hides out in a remote mansion."

"Woah," I said before glancing back at the dick.

I smile broadly at my friends.

"Money can't buy class, ladies." I love rubbing it into them every chance I can get. The girls don't have a title like me. We remained friends from high school to Uni because we were all in the same boarding school.

Cecelia throws me a calculated look.

"He could buy and sell your Daddy a few times over."

I shoot her a venomous look.

Marie raises her hands to get our attention. Cecelia looks over at her, but my eyes remain on Cecelia. She is going to regret her words.

Before I can say anything, the waitress brings my food. I groan. The strong smell of the cheese turns my stomach.

"I've changed my mind. Take it away, please."

She looks uncomfortable, but she picks up the plate and walks away.

"We need to get to a club after this shithole tonight." I groaned to the girls.

Some strategic selfies here and then at the hottest club in the city. My followers deserve only the best.

I make good money off the losers.

CHAPTER 4

Zak

I watch her walk off with her posse with great relish. I can see why she is the ringleader. She is bitchier than the other two. Her mannerisms, posture and posh accent scream rich bitch. They are in their twenties, too young and selfish to care about charity.

It looks as if she is about to bitch about the food that's been put in front of her. Curious, I pull out my phone to see who she is. I'm flooded with links to her social media pages.

I flick through the links pausing at her slutty poses in some of her pictures. I'm sure she is trying to look coy, but she just looks like an upmarket whore to me.

I zoom in on a picture of her wearing a white bikini. Her nipples are practically popping out. She has a nice set of tits. They don't look fake.

4.7 million followers. A self-professed fashion and style icon. No wonder she was so full of herself. I wonder how many of her followers care that she is a cunt?

When I feel eyes on me, I discreetly look toward her table from the corner of my eye and see all three women looking at my table.

I put the phone on the table and sip my wine. Alcohol is something I rarely indulge in, but every so often, red wine is the exception, and it's permissible due to its health benefit.

I look at the banners showing the housing projects. My

mother always smiled and reassured me no matter what happened in our lives. We left our home away from my father to a women's aid housing unit. We ended up in a homeless centre until the local council got us a shitty apartment.

"Mr Henderson, thank you so much for attending."

I glance up to see the director of the foundation. Giving her a nod, I stretch my hand out to shake hers. Keen to get tonight over with, I invite her to sit down.

* * *

As I leave, I see the trio of young women climbing into a black cab. When the cameras start flashing, I hastily get into my limo. Sitting back, I viciously yank my tie off.

Thank fuck, tonight is over.

* * *

I race through my estate I know my timing won't be as exceptional as yesterday, so I push myself harder in the last leg of my run. Being unable to sleep well last night triggered my agitation. I had found myself on Lady Linden's Instagram, Facebook and Twitter accounts.

It irked me to see her posing at the foundation as if she was a modern-day mother Theresa. Picture after picture, I was trying to put my finger on what seemed wrong. She almost looked plastic. I had looked up a children's Barbie doll. She looked like a doll. Her hair just needed to be a little lighter, but she could pass for a human Barbie doll. Even her perky tits match the doll's shape.

All her pictures looked staged in one way or another. After finding her favourite brands and email address, I send some nasty malware programs to access everything. It's been a long time since I've toyed with anyone.

I reach my front door and check my watch. I get my breath under control. Furious at my shit timing today, I take off my cool down jog. I will make it up with my weight training.

I ignore the raindrops and visit my mum's garden. She was too kind for this world. She put up so much abuse from my father.

After she passed away, I cut my father's hands off for raising them against her. He didn't recognise me when I picked him up. I had toyed with him for 18 months and relished every minute of my time with him.

I close my eyes, smiling and tilt my face towards the sky.

Yes.

It's time for a new challenge.

❋ ❋ ❋

I check to see if Benny is online before I send him the amended programme.

Benny: *Thank you. How did I not see it?!*

Me: *You were balls deep in your new girlfriend?*

Benny: *I should never have mentioned her to you. Only the supplier and my credit card company should have known.*

Me: *Just give me today, and I won't mention my future sister-in-law again.*

I see Benny's online icon disappear, and I burst out laughing. Poor Benny. I need to stop fucking with him.

Curiosity gets the better of me, and I look up plastic sex dolls. The scale of them blows me away. Every size and colour you could imagine is available on the market.

Whenever I see a blond one, I compare the silicone doll to Elizabeth. None of them are close to how pretty the real thing is. I pull her picture up, and at that moment, I know exactly what I'm going to do with Lady Linden.

I leave my work and proceed to my favourite section of my home. The conservatory is vast in size, but it's surrounded by glass in every direction. This is where I can think.

I sit in my recliner, feeling the warm afternoon sun on me. Pushing backwards, I tilt the chair back and bring the notepad up on my phone.

She is a Duke's daughter. She lives and breathes in the public eye. My lips twitch at the thoughts that race through my mind. My therapist's words kick in, and I take deep breaths and rein myself back in. It takes several minutes for me to bring my heartbeat back to normal.

No. I need to take my time when I take my pretty doll. She isn't like the others. I will strip her down, rip her soul apart and keep her as a receptacle for me to use, just like an inanimate doll. I ignore my throbbing cock.

I list everything I will need to do, prepare and make a precise timeline of events.

CHAPTER 5

Zak

Nine months later - Hallows Eve

My eyes glance at all the vulgar Halloween decorations on the street. How is this even a holiday? It's cheap and tacky. I only chose tonight because I know exactly what my pretty doll will be doing tonight, getting wasted.

I've compiled everything about Elizabeth over the last nine months. As much as I despised her when I first heard her voice, that's no longer the case. I just need to complete one final task from my list.

I knock on the wooden door. A big ass house, and he doesn't have a doorbell. I'm looking around when I spy his camera.

Eventually, the door opens around two inches, and I hear a chain rattle.

"Open the fucking door, Benny. It's Zak."

"Zak!"

I hear him unchain the door, and my pale skinny friend is wearing a massive grin on his face. His brown hair is overgrown and messy, but he is clean-shaven. He is wearing a blue and black tartan mini robe.

"What the fuck are you wearing? Do you need me to come back? You look as if you were with your missus."

He rolls his eyes at me, but I can see he is happy to see me. It eases any lingering vestige of doubt I had.

"It gets hot, and my mini robe keeps me cool. Do I want to know how you found me? Quick, get in. I am avoiding the trick-or-treaters. I break out in a cold sweat at the thought of people constantly knocking at my door."

He walks inside and waits for me to follow him.

"Close the door and put the chain on. For your information, I now have three wives. I consider them my harem of delight."

I pause, closing the door behind me. No wonder he needs to cool his dick off in that mini robe he is wearing. I chain the door up and follow him down the hallway. Looking around his home. He has done well for himself. He is only a year younger than me.

"You look bigger in person than in your pictures."

My lips twitch in amusement. It's something I hear often. People expect a tech genius to be skinny and nerdy, perhaps if my life had been different, I would have. The daily weight lifting and running are what keep my dark aggression from running rampant.

"Don't worry, your tiny man robe does nothing for me."

We walk into his modern black polished kitchen. I'm surprised his house is spotless. He looks like a hobo.

"Can I get you a drink?"

"No. I'm good."

He sits on the corner couch and nods at me. I'm relieved to see he is wearing shorts when I notice his robe has ridden up his legs. I cringe when I see he has Pokémon boxers on. I close my eyes and pray that I am about to do the right thing.

"I'm going away for a while, and I wanted to proposition you to a job in my company, help me grow and run it. If you do well, I will give you shares in the company."

"Holy shit," he said, running a hand through his messy hair. "Hold on," he said, frowning at me. His eyes narrow on me. "Is everything okay? Where are you going? This is very sudden."

"Everything is fine. I've worked non-stop since my twenties.

It's time to kick back and carve some me time out."

He snorts.

"You're only what? Thirty or thirty-one?" He asked before taking a deep breath. "You know, with my agoraphobia, I won't be able to work on-site."

I nod my head.

"I know, and you won't need to," I said, wanting to assure him it was not an issue for me. I understand better than anyone.

He looks straight at me with a massive smile on his face.

"I'm all in, my friend. I hate my current job. Where do I sign?"

It took me a few hours to run everything by him. The fucker had too many questions and refused to have them answered by my underlings. In the end, I appreciated how thorough he was.

People think I care about my work, my company. It's what cost me precious time away from my mother when it mattered the most.

I had intended to make her life easier with my invention. She never complained once to me. She encouraged me to work hard and to stay focused.

I worked day and night developing my first programme. By the time I finished and went home, she was gone. It was soul-destroying. I missed her by three days.

I flick through all the letters she had left me. Her last words to me. Once I've read through them, I put them in my safe. I won't be seeing them again for a long time. Not even Benny knows how long I will be gone.

Benny will be moving into my home when he can be transported. He had requested that he and his wives be 'taken' while asleep. He turned out to be quite the diva.

I slide the bookcase panel over the safe until I hear the locking mechanism.

It's time to collect my doll.

❀ ❀ ❀

She staggered home at two am. I watched her constant updates in her slutty little witch outfit. She won't be flaunting my body to anyone ever again after tonight. This is her last Halloween in England.

I shift on the branch, trying to get more comfortable. She sits on the bed and takes her shoes off. How she managed to keep herself upright in that state is beyond me. I pull out my binoculars, looking forward to seeing her strip off. She gets up and goes into her bathroom. I tamper my disappointment down, knowing that she is mine after tonight.

She comes out wearing a little white night dress. She is on her phone again. The main thing is that she guzzled down the drugged water I had left by her bedside. She turns her light off, but I can see the glow of her phone. The girl is addicted to her mobile phone. She was the same at her birthday party. Ignoring all the guests that her parents had invited, only to have her face glued to her phone.

I can't control my smirk. Not having her phone will be the least of my pretty doll's problems. She will discover that defying me will have immediate consequences, and none will be to her liking.

I've spent nine months perfecting her training schedule for Elizabeth to become the perfect compliant doll for me.

The last woman I fucked was Jessica over nine years ago. I'm more than ready to have my pretty doll ready and available for me whenever I have the urge to fuck.

I check the time. The drugs will have kicked in by now. It's time.

I stride towards the patio doors, pull my tools out, and open the door before sliding the tools back into the side pocket of the suitcase. I've been to their house several times.

I quietly tread through the house until I reach Elizabeth's bedroom. My heart is thudding louder and louder against my chest, but I ignore it.

I push down on the door handle and then push open her door. The room is dark, but there is enough light from their outdoor security lighting for me to see her tiny form lying in bed. I lay the suitcase beside her on the bed to unzip it. Pulling the covers off her. I scoop her up and stick her in the suitcase. I make quick work of stuffing her arms, legs and hair inside before zipping it up.

On the pillow lay her phone. I grin with the satisfaction of leaving it behind. The amount of extra work that her phone had given me was infuriating. My pretty doll got a lot of male attention.

I hoist the suitcase up and take it downstairs before tilting it towards me and wheeling her through the house until I get outside. Not wanting to make any noise, I lift it up and go through the gardens and climb over the fence before reaching over to pick my doll up.

His Grace has cameras around the property. This was the only blind spot in his security.

Glancing up at the sky, it's a clear night, and the moon shines brightly. I don't put my torch on and haul her onto my shoulder before going through the woods to where my car is parked on a side road close to their estate.

Now to get to the private airport. I need to make several stops before we reach our final destination.

PART II

CHAPTER 6

Elizabeth

The first thing I feel when I wake up is pain. I try to blink open my eyes, but my eyelids burn. The pain stings so much that it makes my eyes water. I feel around my bed to try and get my phone, but I freeze when I feel the pain in my breasts, pussy and fingertips.

What the fuck happened to me?

"Mother? Mum? Daddy? Is there anyone there?"

A large hand touches my wrist, and I sigh in relief.

"Daddy, what's going on?"

I hear a chuckle.

"I am definitely *not* your Daddy." A deep voice said.

I force my eyes open, blinking back the tears. I yank my hand away, but it hurt my fingers.

"Who the fuck are you?" I said as I blinked away the tears to see the man. My lips are stinging.

"I suggest you learn to stop using foul language. I will lay out all the rules for you shortly."

He looks familiar. He is wearing a dark grey hoody and black sweatpants. The man is sitting relaxed on a chair beside me.

"You're Zak Henderson," I said, but my voice cracked. "I don't understand. What do you mean by rules? Where are my parents? Was I in an accident?"

Nothing seems to be adding up. I can only feel brain fog. This feels like a dream. When I look around the large bedroom, it looks like a log cabin. Wait, why does my pussy hurt?

"If you remain quiet, I will tell you everything. I am going to verbalise all the rules, but I have put them up behind the door. It's up to you to learn them. I am not here to baby you."

I feel my eyes widen in shock, but it hurts my eyelid. The fear makes my body rigid. Before he speaks, I know my life has changed. I'm certain there are drugs in my body. I know I went to bed last night.

I shakily lick my dry lips but gasp as I feel more pain. When I glance at Zak, he is scrutinising me.

"First, I will tell you why you feel so—tender."

My immediate reaction is to glare at him but temper the urge.

"You were drugged, and I collected you from your house. We stopped off in Russia. You underwent some procedures. Which I will cover off if you keep your mouth shut and let me talk."

This time I can't control myself I glare at him.

He pulls his hood down, and his hair sticks up at the back. The dark stubble is still on his jaw. His blue eyes are dark with the sinister look he has in his eyes. His lips curl upward to one side in a smug manner. Everything about him makes me angry. He fucking did this to me.

He openly smiles at me.

"In Russia, I had tattoos put on your face one on your pelvis and pussy. Both your nipples are pierced, and you have two tracking chips implanted in you. Your nails have been implanted into your fingertips. Your old birth control IUD was removed, and a new implant replaced it."

My breath caught in my throat, and I exhaled in a series of short breaths. I try to keep myself calm. My brain feels scrambled as I try to comprehend what he has told me.

"Oh, and your asshole was cleaned out. I forgot about that," he said with a grin.

It sinks in that he said he had my face tattooed, and I put my hand on my face.

"Why does it not surprise me that out of everything I said, you are worried about your face?"

I glance at him when he leans over to the side of the bed and passes me a small round mirror. When I look in the mirror, I shudder a breath of relief out and see he hasn't—No. I bring the mirror closer to my face. My eyebrows look darker, and I have black eyeliner, and my lips are tinged in an unnatural pink colour. It's not garish, it reminds me of what my lips look like when I eat cherries. It isn't distasteful, but this was done without my fucking consent.

I pull myself up on the bed and lean against the headboard, ignoring my body's pain. He still looks relaxed in the chair when I look at him, but he watches me.

"What have you done? Do you know who I am?" I said, trying to keep the indignation out of my voice, but it didn't work.

Any amusement he had on his face vanishes. He leans forward, and I automatically lean back into the bed. He looked at me ominously. I gulp and try to sink further into the bed.

"I know exactly who you are. Let me tell you something. We are out in Mongolia, close to the Gobi desert. There is nothing but wilderness in all directions. I am the one who flew us out here. There are no phones, no internet, I am the only one who can fly the plane to pick up supplies. You are welcome to try and leave, but the night temperature dips below minus in some parts, and you will die."

He leans back and gives me a moment for the information to sink in. Not able to keep my eyes on him, I look down at the mirror I put on my lap, and I notice my nails. I try to focus on the nails and ignore what he says. There is no way I can be in Mongolia. Perhaps he is a lunatic. After I met him at the homeless foundation charity, I looked him up on the internet. He is only in his thirties but is a recluse. This must be why. He is fucking nuts.

I refocus on the nails. He said something about implants. The colour matches my lips, and they have tiny white diamantés in them. They look pretty. Maybe this is a dream. No. I can feel the cold air.

A cold shiver runs down my spine, and I pull the covers over my bare arms. I glance down at my chest, and I'm wearing a plain cotton T-shirt.

Trying to understand why he is doing this to me, and my mind comes up with no comprehendible explanation. Keeping my head down, I shoot him a glance.

"Why are you doing this to *me*?"

"I'm glad you asked. You are going to be my pretty little sex doll. We are here so I can train you to my liking."

My head snaps up at his words.

"No! Absolutely not. I am not a fucking whore."

"That's the second time you have cursed. Do it a third time, and you will be punished."

"I am not a *fucking* whore." I said with the words hissed out between my clenched teeth.

He pins me with a feral look but calmly gets off the chair. My eyes follow him as he walks toward the chest of drawers beside a wardrobe.

My bravado is failing me as I can't see what he is doing. His gorilla sized body covers everything from sight.

CHAPTER 7

Zak

This girl is so predictable. I knew she wouldn't be able to control her mouth, and it's the first thing I am going to rein in.

When I turned around, her face was scrunched up in worry. I roll my head and crack my neck before I leap on the bed, startling her into screaming.

I yank her body down and crawl over her until my knees are on either side. Her screaming will make this easier. I push the gag into her mouth until she chokes and splutters.

I can feel the resistance in the back of her throat, but I shove the dildo harder until it pushes past the resistance. I keep a hold of it with one hand and gather the fastening, ignoring her weak struggles.

I climb off her and look at the black leather covering most of her mouth, jaw and some of her cheeks.

Her bright blue eyes are brimming with tears making her eyes shine bright. My dick is rock fucking solid. I must cover the rules with her first before I fuck her ass. I need to wait till the tattoo on her cunt heals.

"That's better." I pat her head then I frown at her hair. It has tangled up in the struggle. I smooth it down with both hands.

My fuck doll needs to look pretty for me at all times. I ignore the sobbing behind the gag. It's just part of the process. I climb off her and sit back down on the chair.

"Focus. I still need to go through the rules with you. You can cry afterwards."

When she turns to face me, I manage to stop myself from smiling. She looks utterly pitiful while gagged and has a defeated look in her eye. Little does she know that this is the beginning of a very long and brutal journey.

"Rule one. You will not talk. You get my attention by raising your hand if you need to ask me anything. If I allow you to talk, I will say speak. The punishment for breaking this rule is a mouth gag in your mouth for two weeks. The one you have in your mouth is the smaller one."

Her eyes widen, and she makes some more choking noises. She will need to get used to having her throat fucked, so the dildo is a gift. I'm sure she won't see it like that yet, but she will when she sees the size of my dick.

I get up to show her the prop for the next rule. I pull out the monster-sized plug for her ass.

"This is a five by eight ass plug. It's made with acrylic and aluminium. I can attach electrical pulses to it."

My dick jerks at the terror in her eyes. The reality of having her here is far better than I could have imagined.

I walk closer towards her so she can see the massive butt plug up close. She pulls the covers over her chest as if the blanket will save her.

"This going inside your asshole if you ever think of refusing sex with me. This is rule two."

I set the plug on the small table beside the bed so she could see it.

"Rule three is if you refuse or do not dress up like my fuck doll. I take away all your clothing privileges."

"Rule four, if you ever use foul language, depending on what you say, it will either be soap in your mouth, my piss down your throat, or you will be licking my dick clean after it's been in your ass."

I ignore her moaning sounds and move on.

"Rule number five, if you don't follow my instructions or do the chores I ask you to do—well, I'm going to leave this punishment open for several things I will do to you. You can use your imagination."

I smile widely now.

"The final rule is if you are miserable or bitchy I will give you something to be truly miserable about. These are your six rules. Any questions?"

I snigger, knowing she can't talk. She glares at me for a second before remembering all the shit I just told her, and she quickly looks down.

"Now, since you didn't know the rules, you only need to wear the gag for five days instead of two weeks."

I don't want to hear her questions and attitude right now.

"As of right now, you are my Fuckdoll. I've not fucked anyone for nine years, so I'm warning you now. I am going to use you every opportunity I get."

She frowns and blinks at me.

"My ex put me off as she was a cheating bitch," I said when another thought occurs to me about Elizabeth.

"If you ever look at another man, you will regret it, Elizabeth. I would make you suffer in ways you could never imagine. Do you understand everything I have told you?"

She sniffs in some air through her nose several times, but she nods at me.

"Good. Now get off the bed, take the T-shirt off and get on your hands and knees. I want to fuck your asshole."

She moves her head as if she is about to refuse, but she stands up and follows my instructions.

She keeps her back to me as she tugs off the T-shirt throwing it on the floor.

"Pick it up, fold it, and put it on the side table."

She doesn't turn around, but she follows my instructions. My eyes run over her body. I have already inspected her body fully. I've had to keep her piercings clean and check for infection.

The medical kit is fully equipped and has several courses of antibiotics if required. But I would rather avoid her getting sick.

I tug off my hoody, T-shirt and yank my sweatpants down. I leave my black socks on because the floor will be cold. My eyes don't leave her as she bends over the bed. Her blonde hair tumbles over her face.

Her pink little pierced tits hang down underneath her. I can't wait to fuck her pussy. I have my name along with some artwork on her pubis, and her outer labia has a tattoo on it. Combined, it says Zak's Pussy with the word pussy on her cunt.

She keeps lifting her hands up and down on the bed. I realise the nail implants will be irritating her. Having her flat on the bed will hurt her nipples.

I glance at the wall mirror on the other side of the room. That's perfect for what I have in mind, and it will show her what a good fuckdoll she is.

I get some lube out of the drawer and throw it on the bed beside her. I stroke my cock looking at her holes. I can see a small part of the black and blue ink on her cunt, making me drip.

Taking the lube, I put some on my fingers and pulled her ass cheek to one side to see the tight wrinkled hole. I push my finger in, making her grunt, but when I glance up at her head, she still has it facing downwards.

The lube causes my finger to slip easily in and out of her ass. I push a second finger inside her, watching her hole strain and stretch around them.

"This is a lovely hole, Fuckdoll. I can't wait to get my cock in here."

She whimpers at my words.

"I'm going enjoy creating my anal slut. You will love taking my fat cock in here," I said, wanting to fuck with her head.

I continue to fuck her asshole with my fingers until her hole feels nice and relaxed.

My sole focus is getting inside her asshole and fucking her till

I cum. I won't last long, given it's been so long since I fucked a woman.

It sure beats wanking off to porn.

CHAPTER 8

Elizabeth

I keep breathing heavily through my nostrils. The gag is hurting my throat. It's so deep inside me that I'm sure it will damage something inside me. I whimpered again when he began to move his fingers inside me.

My ass automatically tightens around his fingers, making it more uncomfortable. He opens his fingers up inside me, and I yell at the stretch I feel. I look to my side and see the giant butt plug he left on the table. I relax against his fingers I never want that thing inside me. It looks as big as my fist.

The longer he continues to finger my ass it begins to feel nice, and I try not to make a sound to alert him to what I feel.

His fingers tighten against my ass cheek.

"That's a good Fuckdoll. Relax your asshole for me." His deep voice sounds deeper with a husky tone to it.

I think back to his words and pray he cums quickly. I don't like anal sex. It's too painful.

He pulls his fingers out, but a few moments later, he tries to push his thick dick inside me. The pressure doesn't let up. And I gasp not only as his head slips inside but as my fingertips ache pressing against the bed covers.

I try and relax my ass for him, so he finished quickly. He pushes another few inches in, and I groan as he stretches me out.

"This is such a tight asshole. You're going to be my perfect pretty Fuckdoll," he said, groaning as he pulled back and thrust into me again.

Please, please, please, please, cum quickly. I chant in my head. My heart is pounding in fear because he feels so large inside me.

He grips my hips and surges deeper inside me. I force myself not to tighten up.

He moans and holds me close to his body. The room is cold, and his body heat feels good.

"Sit up. Get off your hands."

I follow his instructions because it eases the pain in my fingernails. But his thick hands grip my thighs, and he lifts me off the bed. I quickly lean my head back so I don't topple forward. It only sinks me deeper onto his cock.

He walks across to the other side of the room, and I cringe when I see him walking towards the mirror.

He stops in front of the mirror, and I immediately close my eyes. His hands shuffle along till they hold my ass. He begins me lift me up and down his cock. It feels so deep and intense that I moan.

"Open your eyes Fuckdoll," he said.

I can't. I shake my head. He holds me still but slides himself slowly in and out of my asshole.

"Do you know what a Fuckdoll is?"

I don't open my eyes or respond to the crazy fucker.

"You're just a container to dump my cum in. If you don't open up your eyes once I've nut inside your asshole, I will take a long piss deep inside your asshole. I'm going to fill you up and use your holes as my personal little toilet."

My eyes fly open, and I look at his eyes that are above my head.

"Good, Fuckdoll. Now look at your cunt."

My eyes drop down the mirror, and not only do I see myself impaled on his dick. I see his name scrawled all over my pubis area. Zak's pussy, the tattoo read.

He places one hand under my thigh and the other on my ass

cheek.

"Now keep your blue eyes on mine while I fuck your dirty little asshole."

His words make me shiver, but I bring my eyes to him, and I can see the intense need burning in his eyes.

He moves me up and down slowly as if I can feel everything tenfold in this position. I relax each time he impales me on his cock. He shows no signs of tiring as he thrusts his hips upwards, driving deeper inside me.

"You know what's perfect?" He asked, keeping his eyes on mine.

I shake my head. My eyes catch the barbells on my nipples. They are silver with white or pearl balls on either side of my nipples. I swallow on the throat gag when I see them.

"Your cunt is weeping to be fucked," he said with a nasty smirk. "Just like a Fuckdoll should be. Have her holes ready for her owner anytime he needs to dump his cum. Hmm?"

I don't look down or acknowledge his words because I can feel myself getting wet. He looks so powerful, holding me up with ease. He has a large body that I can see clearly because I look tiny by comparison. I feel the tears of helplessness well up.

I look like his fucking doll.

CHAPTER 9

Zak

When her eyes well up with tears, my cock jerks and twitches inside her. I forget about fucking with her head and look at her pussy with my name on it.

"I'm going to fuck this hole open wide. Get used to me pumping my cum inside it."

I slide her up and watch when I drop her on my dick to swallow it all up. The tight hole felt incredible. I tighten my fingers and move her up and down on me. Using her hole like I said I would. I ignore her whimpers and moans. Her cunt is glistening now, but she doesn't deserve to cum.

Not yet.

After six or seven hard deep thrusts, I rush back to the bed, lifting her off my cock I sit her on the bed and push her back on it wanking my dick over her cunt.

"Open your legs wide, Fuckdoll," I pant out. My heart is fucking racing.

As soon as I see her pretty wet cunt lips, I shoot my load on her spraying her pussy, watching it spray her stomach. Her pink asshole is still gaping open, so I shove my cock back inside her, growling when I continue to spurt the rest of my cum inside her asshole.

I slowly slide my dick in and out of her asshole. My cum has doubled up as lube and eases my path. I see some of it leak out, and I pull back to see some droplets drip from her hole. Her cunt and tattoo are covered with my cum. I smile at the sight.

My pretty Fuckdoll.

I can't wait to train her to be my obedient cum-dumpster.

I get a tissue from the table and wipe her cunt. I need to keep the tattoo clean for now. I smile, wiping her arousal. I use the tissue and rub her clit. Her hips jerk, turning my smile into a grin.

"You filthy Fuckdoll. You enjoyed me fucking your asshole. If we go at this rate, it won't be long until you beg me to fill your holes. I might even let you cum next time," I said, removing the tissue from her cunt and tossing it into the waste basket beside the bed.

When I look at the horrified look on her face, my mind goes to when I first met her. It feels damn good to put her in place, but for her to enjoy getting her asshole pounded like a common whore?

That is fucking priceless.

I hear her stomach rumble and remember she needs to eat.

She's earned her first meal.

❊ ❊ ❊

I watch as she demolishes the soup and bread. I remember her being such a bitch about the food at the charity event. She will be digesting some nastiness from me while she is my Fuckdoll.

I'm looking forward to when she misbehaves. My dick twitches again. My eyes go to her tinted lips. The artist did a damn good job on her. She looks like the perfect doll but has no nasty plastic holes or fake silicone tits.

Not my pretty doll.

I finish my soup and decide to test her some more. I want her to fail. I wait until she has finished her food. Due to the temperature, she wears black sweatpants and a red jumper. Tomorrow I will sort out the wood fires. I want to watch her walk about dressed up like my perfect doll.

"Since I cooked your washing up."

I doubt she has washed any dishes before.

"Pick up our dishes and take them to the sink. Use the container of water to wash them and put them on the side to drain," I instructed.

She does as she is told. She used a little too much water but other than that, it's a good first attempt.

"Follow me."

I take her back into the bedroom and sit on my recliner, lifting my book from the table before looking at her.

"Bring me your gag."

She brings it over to me without saying a word.

I motion to her with a finger, and she leans forward for me, the plastic dick deep inside her throat again. I fasten it up tight.

"Get on your hands and knees beside my feet," I said, looking into her confused blue eyes.

I smile.

"I forgot to order the footstool for the chair. So kneel by my feet because that's your job for tonight."

She looks aghast but slowly stands up and does what she is told.

I pull my feet towards the chair and watch her get on her hands and knees before I put my feet on her back. She has curled her hands on the wooden floor to protect her nails. I relax my feet on her back and open my book.

Life is good.

❊ ❊ ❊

The next week goes smoothly, with her being well-behaved enough to have the gag removed. I've been fucking her asshole daily. She can take a hard pounding now. I've not used her mouth hole yet. I'm waiting for her to slip up before I fuck that hole.

Her tattoo and piercing are looking good. I haven't let her go outside yet. I know she is desperate to explore her surroundings. The plane is covered up, and there is the woodshed out there. That's it.

I had this cabin specially built here. It's completely desolate out here. I knew it would be the perfect training ground for my Fuckdoll. I've missed my training routine, so I decided to jog today. The cold morning air will be good for my lungs. The sand, not so much.

"Fuckdoll, I'm going out for a jog. Be a good girl, and don't go outside."

I manage to say this with a straight face because I know she won't be able to resist going outside.

She looks up from the book I gave her. I brought a selection of classic and modern books with me. She won't find the satellite phone or internet connector. I have them stashed in the plane.

She opens her mouth but then remembers. She lifts her hand.

"Speak."

"When can I go outside, please?" Her voice has an annoying whine to it.

"When I say you can."

She purses her lips and narrows her eyes at me but looks back at her book again.

I go into the bedroom and get my trainers before I close the front door, I place two feathers, one underneath the door and one between the door and the doorframe. I ensure the feathers are still in place when I shut the door. The pillows won't miss them.

I do my stretches for a little longer this morning, and I jog on the spot until I spy Fuckdoll peering out of the corner of the window. I pull my hoody up, grinning and take off sprinting.

CHAPTER 10

Elizabeth

I crouch under the window and see he is still jogging on the spot. For fuck's sake, when is he going to leave?

Stay inside my arse.

He pulls his hoody up and takes off running. I stood up because his back was facing the cabin. I quickly put on a jumper and his zip-up hoody hanging on a hook on the bedroom door. The cabin only has four rooms: the bedroom, kitchen, living room and bathroom. It's quite spacious, but not near the luxury I'm accustomed to.

I get my fluffy slippers on because these are the only shoes he has given me.

I look around all of the windows in the house. The land looks so flat outside, and I need to ensure he isn't someplace he can see me.

My heart is fucking pounding as I stand beside the door. I cringe thinking about how he still uses me as his god damn foot every night after dinner. To say he is a giant pain in my ass is an understatement. All he has done all week is fuck me in my ass.

I take a deep breath and push the handle down with a shaky hand.

Damn it! I'm too scared.

I look around the kitchen and see my book on the table. I'm safer sitting my ass back down and reading.

Fuck it. A quick peek won't do any harm.

I pull the door open and look around outside before I step outside. I rushed around the entire house and saw he was telling the truth. My shoulders sag in defeat. There is no escape.

There is a plane and a large wooden shed. The plane is covered up with a large camouflage patterned covering. It's quite a big plane. Then again, he is a billionaire freak. He could afford a fleet of them.

I look at my surroundings and feel as desolate as the land. It's completely barren. Some grassland and sand in the direction where the bastard ran. There are only a few hills or sand dunes. I can't tell because they are too far away. I kick the stupid grass in frustration.

Fucking Mongolia!

How will anyone ever find me? My parents must be worried sick. My friends will be crying fake tears. I don't blame them I would do the same if the same happened to them. Our society is cutthroat. It's a dog-eat-dog world.

I take one last walk around the cabin before going back inside. Taking in the fresh, clean air. It felt good. At least he won't know I had been outside.

I pause at the door, slip out of my slippers, and step inside with my socks on. I bend down and, to one side, smack the slippers together to get all the dirt off them. I don't want to track any sand in incase he spots it.

The guy is OCD or just very precise in everything. I must comb my hair about four or five times daily because he wants it to sit perfectly.

I sit back down at the table and pick up my book with a sigh. At least it's an eco-friendly house, but it has a backup generator if the solar panels malfunction. I don't know what I would do without electricity. Mr OCD told me all the environmental benefits of the cabin he had designed and built. Since I have no phone, TV or social entertainment, I have to listen to him prattle on like the National Geographic channel. It's been a week, and I already miss civilisation.

Fucking Mongolia!

❊ ❊ ❊

He came back from his run drenched in sweat. Thankfully, he never asked if I stayed inside or not. He downed a bottle of water and went straight in for a shower. I was so relieved. Now I'm just agitated.

He made me cook dinner, wash the dishes, and now I'm probably going to be his footrest for the night while his big ass was relaxing on my back. I try not to slam the dishes on the sideboard. I finish wiping everything down before washing my hands. My poor hands are going to dry out and become wrinkly.

The nights are freezing, but it's much better with the wood burners he keeps on now.

I enter the bedroom and quickly close the door to keep the heat in. He is sitting on his recliner like the lord and master.

"Take your clothes off and come here."

I pause to stare at him. This isn't what we usually do. I take my clothes off and fold them up on the chair. Most days, he kept me naked, and I've gotten used to it now. When it's warm like this, it doesn't bother me.

I walk over to his chair and wait for him to speak. He puts the book marker in the book and places it on the table.

"What did you do when I went for my jog this morning?"

I gulp and stare at him in panic. There is no way he could have known. I want to look around the room for cameras, which might make me appear guilty. I clear my throat.

"I read my book," I said.

It felt weird being able to speak.

He lifts something from the table. It's too small for me to

make out what it was.

"On your knees, kneel down."

Confused, I kneel in front of him. I watch as he peels a round tab off. He places the flesh-coloured plaster over my nipple, covering it entirely before doing the same to the other.

His blue eyes darken, and I know my ass will be sore again tonight. He gets this feral look in his eyes. It must be how a lion looks at his prey or a lioness because I don't know if he is going to kill me or fuck me when he stares at me for so long. Exactly, like he is doing right now.

I lick my lips nervously. This is different. I don't like different. It makes him unpredictable.

He stares at me for a few minutes before standing up in front of me, and I'm facing his dick now.

Okay. I think I can handle some of his dick in my mouth. He has used my ass all week. At least my mouth got a reprieve until now.

He pulls his T-shirt off and hangs it over the recliner. He pulls his shorts off completely, with his hard dick bouncing a few times. I cringe at the length of it.

"You were a very bad Fuckdoll going outside."

I feel my dinner churn in my stomach. If I look up at him, he will see my guilty as fuck look, so I stare at his dick instead. The head looks almost purple, and the rest of it looks red. Even his dick looks angry, so I glance at his feet. His feet look normal I focus on them.

"Do you have anything to say to me, Fuckdoll?"

I shake my head. My mind is racing.

How the fuck does he know?!

"I'm so disappointed. You were doing so well."

He doesn't sound disappointed, but I'm not brave enough to look up at him. I wonder if he didn't want his cum on my piercings. He has been very careful with the piercings to ensure they don't get infected.

"Look up at me. I want to see your eyes when I fuck your

42

throat."

I wince at the thought of taking the whole thing. Maybe I can get him off using my hands and a bit of my mouth.

I glance up at him, relieved to see that he doesn't look angry. I keep my eyes on him and open my mouth as wide as possible.

I hope this doesn't hurt.

CHAPTER 11

Zak

I look into her eyes, and for a few moments, they mesmerise me. I've never seen such beautiful clear blue eyes. It makes her look innocent. My lying little Fuckdoll is going to get her punishment. But first, I need to cum using her throat.

I step back a little so I can use the tip to rub it around her mouth. Pausing only to wank a few times to bring up some pre-com. I use it to paint her hot upper lip and rub the rest on her tongue.

"Suck the tip."

She keeps her eyes on me, and her pink lips wrap around the tip before she sucks on it.

"Yeah, suck it harder, Fuckdoll."

I run my fingertips in her blonde hair, running them down to the base of her skull.

"I'm going to push inside your neck, you're going to swallow like you did with the mouth gag. But you keep your eyes on me at all times."

She keeps sucking the tip of my dick, but she nods.

I slide my dick deeper and tighten my fingers in her hair to bring her closer to me. Her eyes begin to water immediately when my cock hits the tight entrance to her neck. Her mouth feels incredible. I can't remember the last time I had my cock inside a hot wet mouth.

I clench my fingers in her hair, and when her mouth slackens from the pain, I thrust hard and yank her head forward. She moans and tries to move back. She makes a strangled noise. I look away from her eyes and see she has another three inches to take.

"Keep swallowing. Almost there, you dirty bitch." I said, moaning towards the end when I felt my balls lurch.

Tears are running down her face now, but she keeps her eyes on me. I pull her off and thrust back inside her, building up a steady rhythm as she adapts to swallowing me each time I thrust inside her.

It isn't long till she has taken me until her upper lip is touching the hair on my pubis.

"Now that's what I call an excellent cock sucking Fuckdoll."

She makes a grunting noise and tries to pull back again. I pull her hair, and she stops.

"I'm going to fuck your throat. Once I'm done emptying my balls inside you. I'm going to keep my dick down your neck and piss directly into your stomach, Fuckdoll."

She begins to struggle against me and choke. I can feel her throat contract around my cock. Her baby blue eyes are begging with me.

"It's your punishment, and if you spill any of my piss out or if you throw up. We do this again until it stays inside you. I will use you any way I see fit."

She lets out a long whine, but the vibrations of it run along my dick, and it only feeds the dark beast in me.

I don't hesitate I pull halfway out and thrust in and out of her neck, pulling her hair to slam her face against me. She struggles to keep her eyes on me as I move her too fast. Each time I fuck down her throat, her lips smack into me.

I pause when my balls rear up, and I feel my cock spray out cum. Her throat felt too good.

"Argh. Oh yeah." I groan before pushing deeper down her throat to give her the rest of my cum. I feel more of it spurt inside her.

Her eyes are twitching, and the tears don't stop falling from her eyes.

"Aaah. Fuck." I breathe out. Feeling my dick pulsate again. Shit. Fuckdoll's mouth was worth the wait.

I keep her on me while I catch my breath. I need to wait till I soften slightly before I can take a piss, so I keep my hands in her hair until I'm ready.

She moans and tries to pull away again. I smirk at her messy face.

"Drink up, Fuckdoll, here it comes. If you don't drink it down, I'll do this again all fucking night."

She tries to shake her head, but I hold her against me. I pull her face closer to me till her nose is squashed up, and I let my flow of piss go inside her.

"Fuck. Oh. Fuck. That feels good," I moan.

My heart races as she struggles to keep drinking my piss, but she has no choice because I'm so deep inside her neck. I pull out slightly so she can breathe through her nose. As she keeps swallowing my hot piss, I feel her throat constrict around me. Her nails are digging into my legs, but I don't care.

When she gurgles slightly, some piss runs out of her mouth, but I still continue pissing inside her. I had been saving it up for her as her punishment.

When I finish, I pull out but leave my tip in her mouth. She pants in small breaths of air and makes a retching sound.

"I fucking dare you to puke up my piss," I warned her.

She moans and holds her stomach. Once she calms the fuck down.

"One last bit since you didn't get a proper taste." With that, I let a little trickle over her tongue, watching it in fascination as she swallows it down.

"You lie or misbehave again, and you'll keep my piss and cum inside your holes for days. Do you understand?"

She nods, and I pull my dick out of her mouth. I put my shorts back on and sit on the recliner.

"Lick the floor up. There is some piss on it."

She looks up at me fearfully but doesn't say anything. When she doesn't move, I pick up my bottle of water from the table.

"I'm going to drink this and piss all over the floor if you don't do it. Then I'm going to make you suck and lick up every single drop of my piss."

She bends down, and I use my feet to slide the recliner back. I'm not missing this for the world.

A Duke's daughter. Lady Elizabeth Linden is on her knees licking up my piss. I let out a chuckle.

"Good, Fuckdoll. Lap it all up. This is just the beginning."

Why would I want a fucking plastic doll? When I have this stunning beauty being my cum-dumpster and toilet.

❋ ❋ ❋

I let her wash up but went into the bathroom with her to ensure she didn't throw up. She spent ten minutes brushing her teeth and tongue, all while giving me daggers in the mirror.

I rub the growth along my jaw. Another week to ten days before her tattoo has healed. She did well tonight. I might let her cum in the morning.

She raises her hand in the air.

"Speak."

"Please, can I take a shower?"

I want to test out her reaction.

"No. You can have one in the morning."

Her shoulders slump down, but she doesn't say anything. We walk back into the bedroom, and I strip naked to get into bed. When she doesn't move to get into bed. I switch the light off and leave her in the darkness.

It's too cold for her not to get into bed. She is only wearing a fluffy robe. I snuggle into the covers and close my eyes.

Sometime later, I feel her slip into bed. I pull her into me. She deserves a cuddle for being such a good receptacle for me. When I feel her robe, I find the tie and open it up, tugging it until she huffs and removes it. I pull her ass towards my stomach and wrap my arms around her.

I fall asleep almost immediately, with my last thought is hoping she slips up again soon.

CHAPTER 12

Elizabeth

His breathing evens out quickly, and I relax, knowing he is asleep. I'm still trying to get a few things sorted in my head.

I like being humiliated and degraded. When he watched me licking the floor, he had a proud look on his face. He hasn't let me cum at all. His words being I had to earn the privilege. He is sleeping I could—no, I can't. The bastard would somehow know.

I sigh. My brain feels so jumbled up. He looks after the tattoo and the piercings with such care. Only to use me like he did tonight. I don't understand him. I wanted to ask about his ex-girlfriend but wasn't brave enough. I was curious to know if that had turned him into this monster.

I didn't taste any of his pee. Most of it went straight inside me. It was only in the end that it tasted slightly bitter when he put some on my tongue.

I try and remember all the punishments he had said that went along with the six rules. I definitely don't want the giant butt plug in my ass. If I push his buttons tomorrow, what will he do? He hasn't threatened me with any physical harm. I rub my legs together, trying to ease the ache inside me.

I'm going to misbehave tomorrow and see what happens. I worry over it before I tire myself out and fall asleep.

✻ ✻ ✻

After breakfast presents the perfect opportunity. I pick up the dishes and leave them in the sink before going to the other side of the kitchen to pick up my book.

He went for an early run, came back, took his shower, and we just had breakfast.

I sit at the table opposite him and open up my book.

"Aren't you forgetting something, Elizabeth?"

I look up from my book innocently and shake my head. His blue eyes darken, and he points to the sink.

"Wash the dishes."

I point at my book and look as if I'm reading. I can feel his eyes on me, but I ignore him. I'm looking at the words in the book, but I'm not reading them. My heart is pounding, wondering what he will do.

"Fine. Have it your way," he said, standing up.

I hold my breath but still don't look at him. He walks to one of the kitchen cupboards and takes a bottle out. I quickly look back down at my book.

He slams the glass bottle on the table with a loud thud, and he picks me up by the scruff of my robe. I squeak and drop my book onto the floor. He pulls my robe off and pushes me down onto the wooden table.

I put my elbows on the table so my nipples don't get crushed against it. The bottle beside me is olive oil.

"You want to play with me, Fuckdoll? Let's play."

He picks up the bottle and pours it down the crack of my ass. He rubs it all over my ass before pouring more on me. When I feel his hot cock in between my ass, I moan.

He slaps my ass.

"Slutty little fuckhole. You want me to fuck your asshole is that it?"

His fingers rub my pussy gently, and he pushes his oily fingers inside me. I push back onto them.

"Fuck. Your holes look so hot."

I feel him push the tip of his dick into my ass.

"I'm going to let you cum, Fuckdoll, but you had best be ready for your punishment."

I nod my head.

He pushes another few inches inside me, and I relax my muscles, knowing he will fuck me hard soon.

"These holes are all mine, Fuckdoll. If you ever let anyone else use your holes. I'm going to kill you."

His hand grips my head up so high I arch my back and push my head back. He twists my head to the side and kisses my lips.

It's a fierce, probing kiss. He shoves his tongue inside my mouth before he slams the rest of his dick inside my ass. I scream out loud.

He pulls off my mouth.

"I never said I was going to make this easy for you," he said before pulling back and kissing me again before he fucked into my ass again.

I was ready this time and relaxed my ass. My moan bleeds into his mouth. His fingers rub my pussy. He pulls away from my mouth again.

"Are you going to cum on my fingers like a needy whore?"

I twist around to look at him. He had the death stare on me. I nod my head. The faintest of smiles appear on his face. He slides three or four fingers inside me and moves them in and out.

If he hasn't had sex for nine years, how the fuck is he doing all this?

He pulls his fingers out and rubs my clit. And my pussy and ass flutters. I need to cum so fucking bad.

"Oh, you horny little doll. You need it bad, don't you?"

I whine and nod my head.

He pulls back slightly, and I feel him pour more oil on my ass. His dick moves back and forth as he drizzles more oil on us.

He slams the bottle down and grips me by the hips. When he moves this time, he gives me deep hard thrusts.

"Good little, Fuckdoll. Taking my cock so good up, your dirty little asshole."

His fingers find my clit, and he strokes me in time with his cock slamming in and out of me. His breathing becomes erratic, and I can feel myself coming apart.

He slams in and out of me so hard that the table begins to move forward. He doesn't stop fucking me, but he pushes his fingers inside me, and I cry out and cum all over his fingers, my ass clenching down on his cock. He thrusts another two times, and I feel his hot cum soak the inside of my asshole.

I'm past caring, and I rotate my hips, wanting to feel his fingers. He pushes them deeper inside me while holding his dick inside me as he continues to cum.

I'm breathing as I've been running for my life. The final vestige of my orgasm makes my pussy flutter around his fingers, and I drop my head on the wooden table.

I feel him pull out, but I don't move off the table.

"I will never get sick of watching my cum drip out of your gaping asshole," he said, slapping my ass. "Squeeze it all out I want to watch your hole drip it all out."

I do as he asks, even if it feels weird. What the fuck? He kidnapped me, tattooed me, pierced me and made me into his doll, and I'm feeling weird about squeezing his cum out? Maybe we are both crazy because I've forgotten what normal is.

"So fucking hot," he groans. "It's almost a shame you must pay the price for breaking the rules."

I sag on the table, remembering my punishment.

Perhaps it won't be so bad.

CHAPTER 13

Zak

I watch my cum drip out of her hole and trickle down her ass and thigh. I'm trying to think about what she did and what punishment I had allocated to match it. Her asshole is distracting mc. I pull her ass cheeks apart and watch her hole spread open.

I reluctantly let go of her oily cheeks and tried to focus on her punishment. I scoop up my cum from her thighs and hole and smear it on my cock. Once I've gathered it all up, I smack her ass.

"Get on your knees and lick your ass off my cock."

Her head spins around, and she has a frown on her face. Good, she isn't supposed to enjoy her punishment.

My cum is dripping off my cock.

"Fuckdoll, if you don't move, all my cum will end up on the floor, and that's what you will be cleaning up."

She jumps up and is instantly on her knees. Her lips wrap around my dick, and she sucks the head of my cock.

I grip her head and look at the ceiling, moaning as her little tongue works around my dick, lapping me clean.

Smiling, I look down at her, and I feel real affection for her for the first time. She might have tested my limits, but it was within reason. I haven't let her cum since she got here. Edging her worked a treat. Her training is coming along nicely.

I stroke her hair as she swallows my cock down her throat,

moving her mouth back and forth, licking up her mess and blowing my dick until I'm hard again. She will be a fine cocksucker soon.

Another week before I can get in her pussy. All those years watching porn to get off and for the nine months looking at various methods of fucking and pleasuring came in handy.

I know her last fuckhole will be worth the wait.

❖ ❖ ❖

We fall into a comfortable routine. If she resents me, it hasn't come out yet. She has grown accustomed to following all my requests, and I keep her dressed in all the various outfits I have chosen for her.

It's mostly short camisole tops with matching G-string panties or corsets with stocking belts. She is constantly on her knees sucking my cock or bent over somewhere, taking my dick up her ass.

She has become more amenable since I let her cum when I fuck her, and I enjoy the feel of her holes when she orgasms.

Her nipples are healing up nicely now. I'm dying to play with them, but they will take a long time to heal.

She might not have noticed, but in such a short time, she is a far cry from the spoilt little bitch I first met at the charity event. I've made contact with Benny. Everything was going well at work, and when I checked what was happening regarding Elizabeth's disappearance, the police were baffled, and the parents were distraught. It's all a farce. It hadn't stopped them from resuming their social activities.

I'm not bothered about any of it. Their callousness will work in my favour to break their daughter down quicker.

There is no way anyone will find us here. I took every precaution possible. She wouldn't be too happy knowing she was in a suitcase for hours.

I glance over at her as she folds all her clothes after taking them off the washing line I had put up between the cabin and the woodshed. I feel the need to blow some steam off.

"Do you want to know how I kidnapped you?"

She looks up from her task. She initially looked curious, and then she frowned and shook her head.

"I will tell you anyway," I said in an attempt to piss her off.

She gives me a dirty look before moving on to folding the towels.

I explained my ingenious plan in intricate detail, especially about the suitcase and how I ruined an expensive suitcase for her by adding air holes in it. The more I talk, the faster her hands move.

"Fuck you and your fucking suitcase. That was my life you took me from, and you're worried about damaging your shitty suitcase?!" she said with so much anger and resentment that she spat the last words of her sentence at me.

I pierce her with a glare thinking about the nine months I spent watching this girl in her life.

"What life was that? You were almost a junkie like your mother. Popping pills, injecting your body with poison to look good. Your father fucks a woman close to his daughter's age. Were you happy being a media whore? Name one thing you have done in the last twenty-five years that has positively impacted anyone's life other than your own. Name one meaningful connection you have made with any human being," I said in an eerily calm voice.

As I was talking, I saw the anger drain away from her as she took in my words. She holds a towel against her chest, her lower lip trembles, and her eyes tear up beautifully with sorrow.

"Tell me. Is there anyone who loves you in your superficial life?"

Her parents have an heir, their son. Either she was a whim or an accident. They tolerated her at best because I saw no love in that house. She had a lavish party for her twenty-fifth birthday, but after everyone left, she sat crying, popping pills and drinking till she passed out.

She sinks onto the bed, not saying a word.

"Your only purpose is to service me with your holes like a good Fuckdoll. Don't you ever forget that I fucking own you." I said venomously. The thought of her leaving me incensed me.

"Because I would kill anyone who tried to take you away from me. If you tried to escape, I would find you and have your legs cut off, so it could never happen again. I know a good surgeon who would operate on you however I need."

When her head snaps up, she looks appalled. I smile maliciously at her.

"I don't need your limbs to use your holes, Fuckdoll. Remember that."

The rage I feel burns like an inferno inside me.

"Take off your clothes," I said in a flat voice.

She stands up, takes her pink camisole off, and pulls her matching thongs off.

"Come here."

I wait till she stands in front of me.

"My name is on your cunt because I own you. Do you need me to put one on your face?"

She gasps and shakes her head. Her hair flies everywhere. I take the plasters from the tables and stick them over her nipples, ensuring they are airtight.

"Follow me."

I stand up and walk through the house. My dark rage refused to leave me. It makes my head thump and ache. It's freezing outside, perfect.

"Kneel on the grass. Keep your legs apart," I said.

I need to see my name on her cunt while ensuring she understands she is mine. I own every breath she takes.

I pull my hood up as a cold gust of wind passes through me. When I look back at Fuckdoll she is shivering. Her teeth chatter, and she rubs her arms to stay warm.

"Open your mouth up wide, Fuckdoll."

She immediately opens her mouth, her jaw trembling from the bitter cold.

I pull my cock out and aim it at her mouth.

"Do you need me to warm you up, Fuckdoll? Give you a nice warm shower of piss?"

Her tears run down her cheeks, but she nods her head.

I hold my semi-hard cock in my hand and aim it at her face and watch as my hot piss splashes into her mouth. It runs down her body. I move it over her face, and she closes her eyes but leans her body closer towards my warm piss. I piss over her tits, watching my rivulets of piss run down to her open thighs. I pause my piss midstream.

"Open your legs."

I wait till I see the full tattoo, and I piss on her cunt. I stop before I empty my bladder. She is drenched in my piss now.

"This is what animals do, don't they? Mark their territory," I said, moving closer and pushing my dick in her mouth.

I push it inside until I feel it slip past her tight entrance and resume pissing inside her throat. I grip her piss-covered hair and hold her in place. I feel some piss come out of her mouth.

"Fucking drink it, or you're staying out here tonight."

Her lips wrap around my cock like a good Fuckdoll, and I finish pissing down her throat, sighing in relief once I've emptied myself. Only then do I feel the darkness leave me.

I let go of her hair and pat her head.

"You'll learn how to be a good little toilet for me, Fuckdoll. You'll learn to love taking everything I have to offer you."

I hope she doesn't think her punishment is over.

❖ ❖ ❖

I waited until she had a shower and blow-dried her hair.

"Take the plasters off. You need to keep your nipples aired."

I watch her follow my instructions, and her pink nipples are hard like tiny pebbles.

"It's time to clean your ass out with an enema."

She looks at me with apprehension clear on her face.

I strip out of my clothes and turn to go into the bathroom.

"Follow me. We need to do this in the bathroom."

I don't look back to know she is following me. I throw a towel on the shower floor. It's a simple open, designed shower perfect for what I'm about to do.

I get the lube out of the cabinet.

"Get on your hands and knees facing the shower."

She drops to her knees, and I see her puckered asshole and pussy. This should be good I drank two bottles of water while she showered.

I get a separate towel for my knees and bend down behind her. I lube up my dick and squirt more on my fingers to push some into her ass. She stretches out beautifully for me now.

"I'm going to fuck my cum inside your asshole, then piss inside you. I will leave a timer for how long you keep my piss inside you before you use the toilet," I said while pushing my third finger in her asshole and watching her ass strain to take me.

"Please," she whispered.

"Bad, Fuckdoll. No talking," I said, pulling my fingers out.

I force the head of my cock inside her. It's always a tight squeeze initially. The thought of my cum and piss inside her makes me feel violent.

I grip her hair, pulling her head back.

"Don't worry, Fuckdoll. At least it's going to be a warm enema," I said before letting go of her hair.

I pull her ass apart wide, needing to see my dick inside her hole. It's not enough pissing on her and watching her guzzle it down. I want it deep in her fucking guts.

Every part of me.

"Hold on. This is going to get rough."

I used her ass to slide her on and off my dick while I lazily gave her long, slow thrusts into her asshole. She loosens up enough for me to increase my pace.

I pull out and watch her asshole close up before shoving myself back inside her. I put a hand on her shoulder.

"Play with your clit, Fuckdoll. I want you to cum while I give you my cum."

I held her steady and saw in and out of her. When I start smacking into her hard. Her asshole tightens around me I fuck her ass violently.

"Cum, Fuckdoll. Let me feel it."

My hand tightens around her. I don't want to smash her pretty face on the shower tiles. She moans and lets out a small cry. I feel her ass suck my dick in deeper, and I slam into her harder. Pushing my full length inside her and close my eyes, moaning as I empty my balls inside her asshole. The thought of my piss and cum inside her makes me spurt harder. I rock against her but don't pull back. I need everything going in as deep as possible.

I take a few deep breaths as my heart rate returns to normal. I see her hand is back on the shower floor. I use my free hand and feel her slippery pussy wet from orgasm. I rub her cunt and fuck her with my fingers. She moves her ass back against me.

"No. I'm done emptying my balls in you, Fuckdoll. It's time for you to take my piss."

I pull my fingers out of her cunt and bring my hand up to her other shoulder and close my eyes as I feel my hot stream of piss inside her.

"That's my good doll. You take my hot piss up your asshole."

She moans in her misery.

I pull back slightly as I continue to fill her up. I don't want it going too high inside her. Pissing inside her ass feels incredible.

"You're such a good hole for me to use," I breathe heavily before moving my dick back and forth.

Towards the end, I have around four inches of my ten inside her. My stream slows down.

She groans loudly.

I chuckle as I continue to piss in my perfect doll.

"Feeling full, Fuckdoll?"

She nods her head with a soft cry.

"Good, I said, it means my piss is going to clean your ass out nicely."

I pull my dick out and watch some of my piss stain the towels. I focus on my task at hand and spray my piss on her ass and pussy one final time.

I watch my piss dribble down her before standing up and putting the timer on.

"Keep it all inside of you till the timer goes off. I'm going to take a quick shower. Stay kneeling on the towel. I will be checking it to ensure you kept it all in."

I watch her take the towels and crawl near the toilet. I turn the shower on. I'm glad I had the foresight to add the water recycling system. We are going to be in the desert for a very long time.

Casting Elizabeth a glance when I go to dry myself off. She is sitting, holding her stomach. She soothed the dark beast within me like nothing ever had since I lost my mother.

Owning a Fuckdoll is the best thing I ever did. One day I will need to thank Benny.

CHAPTER 14

Elizabeth

I've felt restless ever since that night. When people say it's the quiet ones to watch, I think of Zak, who is the epitome of that saying. It was painful to hear him sum my life up like that.

It's been nearly a week since he gave me a urine enema. I run a hand over my face, remembering waiting before I let it all out of me.

The man is obsessed with me, this isn't normal. I guess he did warn me he hadn't been with anyone for a long time.

"Do you want to go for a jog with me tomorrow?"

I turn my head around to look at him. He is reading his book and has his heavy ass feet resting on my back.

He is serious.

"I'm not very good at running. I can barely keep upright on a treadmill," I pouted.

He smiles down at me, and it's not a predatory, evil or smug one. It's the first genuine smile I've had from him, softening his entire face.

"It will get you out of the cabin, and the exercise is good for you."

Is this the same man who threatened to cut my fucking legs off?

I nod before I resume dwelling on how I became a billionaire's footstool and the life choices I made that got me here.

* * *

The following morning I woke up to Zak's face buried in my pussy, and the man knows how to eat pussy.

He pushed his fingers into my ass and sucked on my clit. I grip his thick hair and rub myself shamelessly over his stubble. I can't believe I used to prefer clean-shaven men. He pushes his thick tongue inside me and fucks my pussy with it.

I wrap my legs around his head so quickly that they tangle in the covers. He throws them off both of us, clearly just as impatient as me.

He glances up at me with a smirk on his face.

"Today is the day to open your final hole up, Fuckdoll."

My mouth is so dry at his words that I can't speak.

"I will enjoy using your cunt as my cumdump this morning. I've waited two weeks for this hole."

I'm still speechless when I watch his head go back down to resume loving my pussy with his tongue and lips. I close my eyes and give myself to the sensations he brings forth. The thought of finally having him inside me is too much for me.

I feel goosebumps over my body, bring my hands up, and squeeze my breasts.

"Such a hot Fuckdoll."

I glance down and see him lapping up at me, but he watches my hands. He pushes another finger in my ass, and I can feel myself about to cum—then he stops. When I glare at him, he chuckles.

He licks his lips.

"This hole is only going to cum on my fucking cock," he said before looking down at me. "My fucking cunt," he growled before slapping me hard. He kneels up and glares at me.

"Ow. Shit."

"What did you say, Fuckdoll?"

I purse my lips and shake my head quickly.

"Keep your mouth shut and spread your legs," he said while he stroked his cock.

I do as I'm told because his punishments are so unpredictable.

"I've never seen a prettier cunt than yours, Fuckdoll."

I don't know how he can make me feel beautiful and filthy at the same time.

He rubbed his dick up and down my seam, and I could feel him move easier as he used my arousal as his lube. When he puts the tip inside me, I hold my breath and open my eyes.

He is wearing his, I'm going to either kill you or fuck you expression on his face again.

"Whose cunt is this?" He growls out at me.

I point to him.

"Say the fucking words!" He shouts at me before slapping my pussy again.

"It's yours. I—It's Zak's pussy." I stutter out.

"Damn right, it is, Fuckdoll."

He pulls my legs up and puts them on his shoulders. He looks like a behemoth towering over me. I say a quick prayer for my pussy. It was nice having one while I did.

He drops down on me, and I scream and cover my face, thinking he will fall on top of me. When I've not been crushed to death, I move my hands away and look at him. He has folded me up, and I feel his dick lurch inside me. I can only see the top of his head as he looks down at where we are joined.

His hands are on either side of me, and I feel him thrust forward, and he feels so big. It's been so long since I last had sex. He pulls back and pushes in again. He is taking his time. It can't be enough for him because he pulls back, splits my legs apart, and digs his knees close to my ass.

"I need to watch this hole get used," he said, breathing heavily.

He begins to piston in and out of me like a damn machine. He is looking at my pussy, and I can't take my eyes off him. His eyes are glowing his fingers bite into my legs painfully.

"Use two fingers only and play with your clit. I want to see the rest of the tattoo when I nut inside this hot wet hole," he pants.

I quickly push my hand down towards my clit and use my fingers to press down before circling my clit. I can feel my heart beating erratically in my chest.

He continues to use me, but he feels so damn good. I rub my wet clit harder, needing to cum.

The whole bed is shaking in rhythm to Zak's movements, but never once does he take his eyes off my pussy.

"Oh fuck yes. Fuck. Cum now, Fuckdoll."

I pinch my clit and raise my hips as Zak slams deep inside me. I keep my hips raised, my ass half on Zak's thighs now, but he feels too good. I lose myself in my orgasm as the waves of pleasure run through me. I don't care what he is doing or about to do or where he is going to piss next at this point.

"My fuckhole," he snarls.

He slaps my pussy and gives me a few faltering thrusts as I feel his dick pulsate and his hot seed fills me up.

I throw my head back on the pillow, trying to catch my breath. He has to be lying. He can't be this good in the sack, not to have fucked in the last nine years.

I feel his fingers release my legs, and I sigh in relief as the pain eases. It didn't feel as bad when he was fucking me.

He collapses on top of me I don't get scared this time because he catches himself with his hands again.

"I knew this was going to be the best pussy I'd ever have," he murmurs.

I look at him with curiosity and raise my hand.

"Hmm. Since your cunt hole was so good, you can speak."

I roll my eyes before I ask my question.

"How did you know?"

He raises his head to look at my face. He looks into my eyes before his gaze drops down to my lips.

"You love being used and abused because you're as damaged as I am."

I frown in confusion. That doesn't make any sense to me. I'm not damaged. I can't deny I've enjoyed some of the things he has done to me.

He lowers his head again and rubs his stubble against my cheek.

"Don't worry your pretty little head about it. I will explain it to you one day."

I think the genius has a screw loose.

✻ ✻ ✻

I genuinely did try to get out of running this morning. I even told him he might have broken my pussy, but he inspected me and said I was fine. I smile, remembering when he winked at me and told me he would break my pussy tonight.

The cold air is rushing into my lungs, causing shivers to run down my body. How can I be so hot and freezing at the same time? And why is he running like a machine, and I'm a panting mess?

I stop and put my hands on my knees, bending over, trying to catch my breath.

When I raise my head, he is jogging on the spot like a fool.

"Come on. You can do more than that," he said while looking at his watch. "It's only been one mile."

I look at him in horror. Do I have to run back a whole mile?

I shake my head at him.

"I will give you a piggyback home if you run some more."

I think about it and decide it is worth it. The thought of running all the way back is awful. It does feel nice to be outside. He is so big I might enjoy the view while he carries me back.

"Did I mention you will owe me if I jog carry you back?"

I scowl at him.

Of course, there is always a *catch* with him.

CHAPTER 15

Zak

My mind has been everywhere today. Besides my mum, I have never shared as much time with anyone like this. I had shared accommodation with a few guys at Uni when I was with Jessica. We had separate dorms. Today had felt comfortable and natural.

I glance at Elizabeth, and she is sound asleep. Each day she becomes more compliant, and I can see her real beauty beginning to shine through. I never in a million years thought she would enjoy getting pissed on. How am I supposed to punish her if she is getting off on it?

When I told her, she was broken. She doesn't know I saw everything she ever typed on her phone in her cloud drive. She has passed through some dark times. If I hadn't taken her, she would have overdosed or led a false life, married and ended up like her mother. She lived a meaningless life.

I snigger quietly.

I'd like to think I've given her some purpose now by being my set of holes to use.

Another thought occurs to me. I swallow hard, thinking about losing her. I will need to carry on with my original plan.

It's the only way.

❊ ❊ ❊

"There are cookbooks here for a reason," I said dryly.

The food is fine. I just need to piss her off.

She slams the wooden spoon on the counter. I chew the inside of my mouth to keep a straight face. I continue to eat my food and ignore her stroppy ass.

"Did you use *any* seasoning at all?" I asked with a faux grimace on my face.

The chair scrapes as she pulls it back to sit down. She has the same as me, chicken with vegetables and some couscous.

I push my plate towards her.

"Here, do you want mine?"

She glanced down at my plate before glaring back up at me. She moved so fast I didn't even see the plate coming.

I wipe the tomato chicken and chickpea mixture off my face to give her a death stare. I don't see one iota of fear on her face.

She looks shocked for a moment before she starts to laugh hysterically. Tears are running out of her eyes, and she is pointing at my head.

I dip my head forward and shake my hair over the table. Pieces of couscous and vegetables fall out and scatter across the table.

I calmly stand up and walk around the table.

Her laughter dies when she realises the danger she is in. She raises her hands as if to pacify me. If I want her to be the perfect doll that will never leave me, she will have to learn the hard way.

"I'm sorry," she squeaked out.

I slam my hand on the table, watching her jump.

"That's two rules you've broken, Fuckdoll. Is this what you need? To be punished? I'm more than happy to help."

I grip a handful of her hair and drag her towards the bedroom where I had set up everything a few hours ago. My Elizabeth has a short temper like myself. It makes her so much easier to manipulate.

Using her hair and my hand on her ass, I toss her onto the bed.

"Don't move," I snapped at her.

She lands face down on the bed. I watch her for a moment, and she doesn't move. She kept her face on the bed. I can't see her expression because her hair has fallen over her face.

I move around the room, getting everything I need. When I get back to the bed, I smile when I see she is in the position I left her in.

I climb on the bed and pick her up by her waist. Placing her head on the pillow, I turn her around. I used the cuffs I attached to the bed to restrain her wrists. I tug at them to ensure she won't be able to get loose. I take the slightly longer ones and wrap them around her ankles.

I adjust the straps so they wrap on the outer part of the wooden headboard. I push them further down to keep her legs wide apart. I climb off the bed to view my handiwork.

"One more thing since you can't control that mouth of yours."

I get a silicone dildo gag. This one is a little under four inches. She will wear it for two weeks so I won't use the longer one. I lightly slap her face till she opens her mouth. I push the navy dildo into her mouth. I will miss seeing her pouty thick fuck me lips, but this is for the greater good. After buckling it up tight, I sit back on the bed and look at her face.

"You look good with a plastic dick sticking out of your mouth."

The gag isn't flat on the outside like the last one. Seeing it stick out of her is fucking hot. My Fuckdoll will know what it feels like to have all three of her holes stuffed tonight.

"Do you think you can get away with breaking my rules and I won't do anything? That I'm a fucking idiot?"

Her eyes widen in shock, and she vehemently shakes her head.

"Do you remember what I said about what a Fuckdoll is?"

She blinks rapidly before nodding her head.

"In the next two weeks of your punishment, you won't ever

I use my lubed fingers and push against the puckered hole watching as her hole strains against me before it gives way. I shove two fingers inside, forcing the small hole to stretch out. I give a couple of thrusts before adding a third finger in. It doesn't take me long until I fit all four fingers inside her hole. I hold them inside her, keeping the pressure against the rim.

"You're damn lucky I am stretching your hole out, Fuckdoll."

She nods with a whimper.

After several minutes I pull my fingers out and see her hole gape beautifully. I quickly pump lube into her open hole. Some of it goes on her cunt and around her ass in my haste.

I take the plug and glance at her face. She looks at the plug in fear, and she shakes her head.

"Perfect. That's three rules in total you have broken. Rule one, no being pissy or miserable. Rule two, no talking without raising your hand and rule three, you just tried to refuse me using your asshole. You just increased your punishment to three weeks, Fuckdoll," I said, watching her eyes widen.

"I would have had less trouble with a silicone doll. After all the time and money I have spent on you. Perhaps if you can't adhere to my six simple rules, I will kill you and leave you buried in the desert," I said, watching her silent crying become full-on sobs.

Looking down at her hole, I see it has almost closed up again. I smear more lube on the plug's tip and push it against her hole. It doesn't look as if it will fit.

I slowly keep increasing the pressure against her asshole, and slowly but surely, her hole gives way. I need to take it out and apply more lube eventually, I get halfway. I ignore her moans and tears but look into her eyes when I push the rest of the plug into her with a final hard thrust.

She cries out loudly. I know there will be no damage. It was just the fear of it being inside her. I must have used half the tub of lube on her. She blinks her eyes a few times but stops her whining.

"Does your asshole feel full, Fuckdoll?"

She nods her head.

"Whose asshole is this, Fuckdoll?"

She tells me through the gag, and even though her voice is distorted, I know exactly what she said.

"That's right. I can use any of your holes with anything I want, any time of the day. You need to get that in your head if you want to continue to breathe."

I clench and unclench my jaw until my back molars hurt, but I continue to glare at her. I will do whatever the fuck it takes to keep her as my doll.

I get some tissues and wipe down the metal part of the plug. I set the charge to low, put the two leads on the metal part of the plug and watched her ass struggle as the electricity current ran through the metal strips of the plug. Her muffled screams make me smile. This is just a normal sex toy from an online retailer. You would think I have sent a full current of electricity through her body.

There are plenty of toys in my arsenal of weapons for my pretty fuckdoll. I've thought of nothing else for close to a year.

Once her screams die down to whimpers, I give her a few last shocks before focusing on the hole I'm about to fuck. I push my fingers inside her pussy and feel the shape of the monster plug against my fingers.

"Do you know how fucking tight this cunt will be when I fuck you?" I said, glancing at her.

Pulling my fingers out, I spit on her pussy before I tug on my cock a few times. Seeing her ass stretched out and her pussy ready to fuck is too much for me. I grab some lube and rub it on my cock before I push the head of my dick inside her. I rub the tattoo on her labia before rubbing her clit. If I'd had the patience to wait, I'd have gotten her cunt pierced with some pretty jewellery on it.

With her holes left open for my use, I place one hand on the headboard and grip her hair with the other. I lift her head so she can watch herself being used.

"Watch me, Fuckdoll. This is what you are, a set of holes for

CHAPTER 16

Elizabeth

I remained awake most of the night, not understanding why he flipped out so badly. Yes, I lost my temper and may have broken the rules, but he was cold with me. His demeanour was different. He left my hands tied to the bedpost but removed my gag. When he brought me my food, he wiped his cum off me, only to add it to my plate before feeding it to me.

I freeze when I feel him shift beside me. He leans over and unties my hands.

"Kneel on the floor, I need a piss," he said with his voice sounding half asleep.

I think of the massive plug, climb over him, and kneel on the floor. He sits up and stretches out for a moment.

"Open your mouth."

I opened my mouth, and he pushed the head of his cock into my mouth.

"Wrap your lips around me. I don't want you dripping any out," he said before giving me a hard look.

I wrap my lips around his dick, and I feel the hot stream splash into my mouth and down my throat. I resist the urge to gag and try to keep up with the stream swallowing it down. Trying my best not to taste it.

Some of it dribbles out as it is too much. I glance up at him, but his eyes are closed, and there is an intense look of pleasure on his face. He opens his eyes and looks at me with a smile.

"I'm done. You're becoming a good little toilet. Lick me clean."

I suck on his tip, but I feel him harden in my mouth as I suck and lick him.

"Get on the bed and lie on your stomach."

I follow his instructions, and he fastens my hands to the bed.

"You're staying tied to the bed today. You need to learn your purpose."

He pumps some of the lube left on the bedside table from last night.

"Your asshole should be nice and loose for me this morning," he said with a drawl.

His hands wrap around my thighs as he parts my legs. Without any preamble, he pushes the round head of his cock in my ass. He doesn't move for a moment. Then he slowly pushed deeper. He paused before fucking in and out me with just the tip.

"So fucking tight even after having the punishment plug inside you."

I feel him move on top of me. His legs move over mine before he thrusts deeper inside me. I moan as I feel him stretch me out. But his dick is a relief compared to the massive butt plug he had in me yesterday.

"Such a tight little fuckhole for me," he growled. "Lift your ass up, take all of me, Fuckdoll."

I arch my back and raise my ass for him. He groans and fills me up with his thick cock. Before long, he is sawing in and out of me. He continued for so long that I was worried.

"Ready for your second load for the day, Fuckdoll? This is how I'm going to use you for the next three weeks," he pants out.

I whimper but nod my head.

"Yeah, take it up, your filthy asshole."

He slams down on me hard, only to pull out and slam back into me. He does this several times before he pushes deep inside me, and I'm almost crying in relief when I feel him cum inside me with a roar. He grinds his balls against me, and his cock jerks as more of his cum unloads inside me.

He stays on top of me, panting heavily.

"Fuck, that was good," he said with a sigh.

He pulls out, but I feel him push a small plug inside me.

"You're getting an enema full of my cum today, Fuckdoll. I will be back when I need to unload again. Be good," he said with a chuckle.

Shocked at his words, I turned around to look for him, but he had left the bedroom.

❊ ❊ ❊

Zak fucked my ass another three times. After each meal he fed me, he would fuck me. Before I fell asleep that night, he told me it was my pussy's turn tomorrow.

❊ ❊ ❊

I started my period a few days later, so he fucked my ass and mouth for a week. He kept me tied to the bed and only came in to feed me or fuck me. He gave me two toilet breaks throughout the day and one shower. By the third week, I was past caring about what he did or how he used me. Sometimes he made me cum. Other times he used me for his pleasure. I just wanted the punishment to end.

❊ ❊ ❊

I know it's the last day of my punishment today. I've behaved so well that he stopped using the gag on me. He took me in for a shower first thing in the morning, which was unusual.

"Sit in the shower, open your mouth and spread your legs."

I do as he asks, shivering a little from the cold tiles on my ass.

"Open your mouth for me."

I open my mouth, and he pulls his shorts down and begins to piss on me. I quickly close my and feel the warm piss soak my face, and hair and land in my open mouth. He moves down to my pussy, and I feel his hot stream on me.

When he stopped, I open my eyes.

"Come here."

I crawl closer to him.

"Open your mouth for me, Lady Linden," he said with amusement clear in his voice.

With my face dripping wet, I opened my mouth, and he pushed his dick inside my mouth. I know what he wants, so I relax my throat and feel him slip deeper inside me.

"You're such a good piss whore for me," he said with a groan as I felt his hot stream resume.

I close my eyes, not wanting to acknowledge his words. I'm grateful when he stops, but he holds himself inside me. When his cock begins to swell and harden, he pulls out of my throat. I stare at his dick momentarily before looking down at his feet. I don't understand why I enjoy him using me in such a disgusting manner. Blinking back my tears, perhaps it's best not to think anything at all.

"Now, you can shower."

I glance at him, and he is standing there watching me. I don't know what for. I stand up and turn the shower on. I quickly wash everywhere, and when I get out of the shower. He is still standing watching me.

"Dry your hair and go back to the bedroom."

I nod my head and towel myself off. He hasn't given me any clothes for the last three weeks. It has helped heal my nipples faster.

I've been so bored because he left me tied up without a book or anything else to occupy my time with. A heavy sigh leaves me. I can't go through another punishment like this again.

When I return to the bedroom, Zak sits in his recliner seat.

"I need to use your mouth, Fuckdoll."

I try not to cringe as I've just taken a shower. Once I stood before him, I dropped to my knees and opened my mouth.

CHAPTER 17

Zak

I've been watching my pretty doll carefully over the last three weeks. Towards the end of the second week, her spirit was at the point of breaking. The third week was when she looked at me in true subservience. Today is her last day of punishment, and I want to make it count because I feel it will be a very long time till she requires correction like this again.

She walks into the bedroom after her shower. My eyes greedily rove over her naked flesh I just pissed all over. My cock is rock solid looking at her pierced pink nipples, her smooth stomach and her hips flare out, inviting me to look at her fuckhole with my name scrawled over it.

"I need to use your mouth, Fuckdoll," I said, but my voice came out hoarse with need.

If I wasn't watching her with such scrutiny, I might have missed the slight grimace on her face. I know exactly how to punish her for that slip-up.

She walks towards me robotically and falls to her knees before opening her mouth for me to fill with whatever I want.

Keeping my eyes on her, I stand to pull my shorts off before hanging them over the recliner. Her hot pink lips will always have that rogue tinge to them, making my cock twitch in anticipation.

I grip the base of my dick with my fingers and thumb and wank it up and down. Her clear blue eyes watch me, and I can see she is relieved that I'm not going to piss inside her. When I see a sticky strand of pre-cum dripping out of my cock I move the tip of my cock and rub it around her open lips, making her pink lips shine.

I grip my cock with my palm and wank harder with some rotation in action to produce more pre-cum I watch it drip slowly into her open mouth.

"Thank me for lubing your hole, Fuckdoll."

"Thank you for the lubricant," she whispered.

She opens her mouth wide for me again. It's the first time she has spoken in three weeks.

"Stick your tongue out for me. I need to fuck your throat this morning."

As soon as I see her wet tongue, I push the thick head of my cock inside her mouth.

"You'll lick my balls with your tongue once I'm in your neck."

I pull her hair into a ponytail and push her down on my cock. Her hot mouth swallows me up, and her throat offers little resistance as I force my dick halfway down her neck. She breathes heavily through her nose in little pants.

I keep a hold of her hair and grip the base of her skull and rapidly fuck in and out of her mouth hole. I feel her dribble all down my dick and balls as I skull fuck her. As soon as my balls smack her chin.

"Lick my balls, cocksucker," I snarled at her.

Her throat constricts as she swallows me deeper before I feel her wet little tongue lick my balls as she moves her tongue back and forth.

My grip tightens around her pushing her face into my pubis. She makes a choking sound, and her throat tightens around my cock. I resume fucking her neck in quick sharp thrusts until my balls jerk as they tighten.

"Fucking hell." I gasped out.

I pull out of her throat, pushing her away from me, and I point my cock to the floor wanking hard and fast. I moan, picturing her ass in the air as she licks my spunk from the dirty floor.

I cum so hard my cum shoots across the floor and her knee. I pull back and watch rope after rope of cum land on the dark wooden floor. I grip my dick and squeeze the tip to let the last few drops drip on the floor.

She is lying on her side from where I pushed her away.

"Lick it up, Fuckdoll," I said, breathing heavily.

She gets on her hands and knees, crouching low as she licks up my cum. I watch her tongue slide in my cum as she laps and sucks it into her mouth from the floor.

I walk around to her ass and kneel behind her. My cock is still hard, and her hole should be wet. The good Lady loves being degraded.

I push inside her slippery cunt, holding her ass up in line with my dick. Her wet cunt swallows me, and her pink asshole looks inviting but fuck, getting up to fetch the lube. I lean over and push her face into my cum. My dick jerks in her cunt as I see her face lying in my cum.

"Did I tell you to stop licking? Lick up every last drop. I want my floor polished clean."

Her cunt ripples around my dick, and I feel a warm gush of liquid coat my cock.

"You love being a dirty little slut, Elizabeth. Your wet cunt doesn't lie," I said triumphantly.

She says nothing, but her pink little tongue comes out, and she laps up my cum.

"Good girl. Lap it all up. Lick my floor till it shines," I said, giving her hole what it needed as I fuck my dick in and out of her.

"Such a good hole, keeping it nice and wet for me."

She moans and lifts her head up, and rapidly licks up my cum stretching her head to reach more. It's the hottest thing I've ever seen, bar my name on her cunt.

I place my hands high on her ass cheeks and grip her soft flesh to move her in rhythm with my thrusts. I groan as I feel her soft insides swallow my dick up. I look down and see her wet slick covering my dick.

"Good. Fucking. Hole," I said each word with a hard powerful thrust.

Her face was being dragged along the floor and in my cum, but I continued to ram her cunt, and I found her clit rubbing her wet pussy until she reared backwards against me and cried out as her pussy exploded around my dick.

I hammer through her orgasm, chasing my second nut, and just as I feel my dick twitch, I pull out halfway and fill her pussy hole with more cum. I pull back a little more and let my final load of cum spurt inside her.

I pull out of her and slide my dick along her asshole. Sadly, that fuckhole will need to wait till lunchtime.

Placing a hand on her back, I stand up to get my shorts back on. Glancing back at her, she moves along the floor to finish licking up my cum. I sit on the recliner to watch my personal Fuckdoll show.

"Stop. Squat down on the floor. I want to watch my cum drip out of your pussy."

She glances up from the floor and bites her lip before awkwardly squatting on her legs with her ass hanging low.

"Wider," I snap at her when I can't see my name on her cunt properly.

She shifts her feet sliding them on the floor until I see her pussy. Her pretty hole is gaping slightly, and my cum is already dripping out of her hole and forming a lovely puddle underneath her.

My body relaxes in the leather recliner. I stare at my pussy for at least ten minutes. I won't even try to understand my obsession with Elizabeth. All I know is I will do whatever it takes to keep her enslaved to me as much as I am to her.

"You're done for the morning after you finish licking your mess up from my floor," I said, glancing at her face to catch her relieved expression.

I watch her ensuring she licks up every last drop of my cum before I leave to make breakfast.

I have the rest of today to remind her of what she is.

PART III

CHAPTER 18

Elizabeth

Halloween one year later

When I hear the plane in the distance, I run outside and can see Zak's plane moving ever closer towards our home. He told me he would bring me back a special present. I'm normally dubious about his intentions, but there was nothing sinister on his face or the tone of his voice to indicate it would be something to torment me with.

As he flies the plane closer to the cabin, I close the door because the sand blows everywhere when he lands to park it. I learn that the hard way. I quickly strip my top and leggings off in my haste I don't bother folding them, but I hang them neatly on the back of the chair.

As soon as Zak opens the door, I run from the table and jump up on him. He caught me and hiked me higher up his body until his mouth was on my nipple. He sucks the barbell into his mouth with a growl. I wrap my arms around his head, pulling him closer as I rub my pussy on him.

He walks in and kicks the door shut before slamming my back on the wall. His hand grips my ass as he struggles with his trousers.

"What the fuck have you been doing?" He said, snarling at me.

I shake my head at him and point to the food I had been

prepping.

He looked at the counter and then smiled at me.

"My horny little slut. You need to ride my dick?"

I nod my head.

He finally gets his pants down, and he rubs the head of his cock along my pussy a few times before he pushes the tip inside me. He moved his hands under my legs and yanked them over his arms. I cry out, but the wall is safely against my back. He brought his head down to kiss me before he moved his ass and fucked me with short hard thrusts. My shoulders scrape against the rough wood with each thrust, but he feels too good inside me for me to care.

He brings his lips to mine before nipping at my lower lip. I feel his hot breath on me as he pants. One hand dips down my ass, pushing his finger into my asshole.

"My Fuckdoll. You always have your holes ready for me," he said against my mouth.

He wrapped his other hand around me and carried me on his dick to the bedroom. He fell on the bed with me beneath him, furiously pounding in and out of me, slamming inside me painfully. I cry and moan, gripping his shoulders and digging my nails into his hard muscles.

"Is this what your cunt needs?"

I hold on tight and nod, unable to speak. Not that I have his permission to.

He raises his arms and slows down to grind himself deeper inside me. I feel his balls rub against me.

"Cum on my dick, Fuckdoll," he said before speeding up his thrusts again. He moans against my breast before he tugs on my barbell. He sucked my nipple into his mouth, and he hit me deep with his cock I screamed as I cum so hard that I'm sure my soul left my body. I arch my back and push my pussy up for Zak. I want his cum.

He is panting hard and fucks me faster until his head snaps up and his eyes are closed, his lips parted, and I feel him empty himself inside me. I wrap my hand around his neck and enjoy the feel of his thick cock inside me. It was a long six-hour wait.

He moves his arms to drop my legs. I feel too lazy to move. He can do whatever he wants, which he does often.

He pulls me on top of him as he rolls onto his back.

"I should go away more often."

I glare at him. Why is he fucking with my afterglow?

He slaps my ass and chuckles. His hand trails up to my hair, and he pulls me down and kisses me long and hard. I feel his dick twitch inside me again, and I rotate my hips, pushing myself down his length.

He nips my lower lip in his mouth before lifting my head.

"You must really want your surprise gift."

Oh, I forgot about the gift. I try to climb off him, but his hands grip my ass.

"I didn't say you could get off my cock, my dirty whore. It's your anniversary gift," he said softly.

I glance down at him in confusion.

"It's been a year since I took you on Halloween," he continued.

I blink at him. It's been a year since we have been in this desert? It didn't feel that long. I should have kept count. He flew once a month to bring our supplies in. I lick my lips nervously. I hope he isn't going away anywhere I hate it when he leaves for hours. It always made me wonder if he would come back for me.

"It's time we moved, and I want your birth control implant removed. It's time to breed your pussy."

I gasp at the last part. A baby. I would love to have a child. It got lonely here. Zak isn't massively talkative. He jogs every morning and likes to read his books in peace. I tried trekking with him once, but the terrain was too harsh for me. The sand, wind and cold were not kind to my skin.

I grin at him and nod my head.

"I wasn't asking, Fuckdoll," he said with a wink.

I roll my eyes at him. We are leaving the fucking desert and having a baby. Best Halloween Anniversary ever. I pause, thinking about what I used to do on Halloween, and I can't help but cringe. The amount of drink and drugs I would consume had left me in a few precarious situations.

I glance down at Zak. I'm ready to move on.

* * *

I look in the mirror. It feels strange to wear full-length clothes again. Wearing a bra was the worst. Since my nipple piercings were poking out, Zak told me to go get a bra on. Muttering about other men wanting to look at my tits.

My face resembles a made-up doll, but I've gotten much healthier. My cheeks have a rosy glow instead of looking pale and almost gaunt. My breasts have gotten slightly larger along with my hips. I still hate running, but Zak made me do it twice a week, which wasn't overly cumbersome.

"We need to leave, Elizabeth," Zak shouted.

I look around the bathroom towards the shower. We have had some damn steamy times in there. Zak is as twisted as they come, but I've grown to love it all and more.

I'm a little scared of leaving. This has been a peaceful haven, albeit a boring one at times, but it was safe.

I sigh, wondering what the future holds for our new location. Zak has been tight-lipped about it.

* * *

Zak flew us out to Ulaanbaatar Airport before we switched to a larger plane. He kept me either next to him or on his lap the entire time. My new fake passport is under the name of Elizabeth Henderson.

The more time I spend with Zak in the real world, I realise

how possessive he is. He kept me close to him as we walked to our hanger his arm went around me if any other man approached, and he terrified the poor steward on the plane.

I snuggle up on his lap and rub my ass on him. He peers over his sexy black glasses and pulls his attention away from his book.

"Your pussy is going to have to wait till we land."

I raise my hand, and he nods at me.

"Don't you want to show *him* who I belong to?" I said, nodding my head towards the steward who was keeping himself at the staff section of the plane.

He slaps his book down, and he is about to take the glasses off, and I grab his wrist to stop him. He smirks at me but leaves them on and drags me into the plane bathroom.

I might be his Fuckdoll, but every once in a while, I get exactly what I need.

* * *

When we land, and the plane door opens, I feel two things. The humid heat in the atmosphere and his cum pooling in my panties. I look around at our exotic surroundings. It's a far cry from a barren desert. We reached a large black car, and I looked at Zak with open curiosity, but he simply held the car door open for me.

CHAPTER 19

Zak

When we reach the port Elizabeth still looks desperate to ask where we are going. I don't know if it is stubbornness or her doll training, but she doesn't raise her hand to ask a question.

After her three-week punishment, there have only been minor infractions since. She looks healthier than the snooty socialite I picked up. I never felt the need to have children, but spending a year with Elizabeth made me realise I won't ever be with anyone else.

I began to resent the implant in her arm, blocking my seed from infecting her womb. The thought of her body swelling up with my seed has been incessantly on my mind for the past four months.

I see a boat crew member looking at Elizabeth in an appreciative manner. I glare at the fucking cunt and pull her closer to me, tucking her under my arm. She grunts as her body hits against mine hard. I keep staring at the cunt until he notices me, and I send him a venomous look. He looks away quickly. I would have zero qualms about slitting his throat and throwing him overboard.

She looks up to frown at me, but I ignore her. There is no need for her to know how fucking crazy jealous I feel whenever another man is around her.

I help her onto the boat, and we wait until the staff have loaded our belongings. Mongolia had done what I needed it to. My island was always my long-term plan, but I needed to reprogram Elizabeth before introducing her to luxury again. I would have ended up killing her or ruining her if she had remained a spoilt bitch.

When I see Esme Island, peace descends upon me before a twinge of sadness hits me. I named the Island after my mother. She would have loved Elizabeth. She never said much about Jessica, and my mother would always speak kindly about people. I must have more genes from my father, which is why I never wanted children—until Elizabeth.

I feel Elizabeth put her hand on top of mine before pushing her fingers through mine. She looks at me with a worried look on her face.
"It's nothing," I said before giving her a ghost of a smile.

I close my eyes and raise my face towards the sun. I am so glad to see the back of the desert.

❊ ❊ ❊

The boat docks on the small pier, leaving as soon as our baggage is taken into the house. I smile as Elizabeth is running from room to room in the house. She screeches in delight, and I know she has found the fuck off massive bathroom.

My crazy Lady Linden is a lover of golden showers. My dick hardens thinking of everything I'm going to do to her in the hot tub. I need to get all my sick shit out before she falls pregnant. I would never risk her or the baby's health. A baby who I hope is just like my Elizabeth.

There is no escape for my Fuckdoll on this Island. I checked the time I have sixteen hours before the doctor comes tomorrow to remove her implant. I'm going to make them count.

I drop my laptop bag on the sofa and jog up the stairs, and she is in the doorway of the master bathroom.

"Like it, Fuckdoll?"

She nods eagerly before she jumps on me, her dress climbing up her legs.

"It's been a while since I gave you an enema. Let's clean your hole out," I murmured in her ear.

A shiver runs down her back. My cock is rock hard and sticking out like a tent in my linen trousers.

"Why don't you climb off and lick your cunt juice off my cock first?"

I slide her down my body, and she unzips the white dress. After it slides on the floor, she picks it up and folds it up, laying it on the bed.

I smother a smile. That is some damn fine training right there. I unbutton my shirt watching her as she reaches behind her back to unhook her bra. She keeps her eyes on me when she pulls it off and puts it on the dress. When she hooks her thumbs on her tiny lace panties to pull them down, I shake my head while pulling my shirt off.

"Leave them on," I said in a husky voice.

I want to peel those down her thighs and uncover my name. I lay my shirt on the bed and unfasten my trousers.

She swallows and rubs her thighs together.

"My Fuckdoll is never satisfied. I should keep all of your holes stuffed up for the next few days."

I glance at the bed. The restraints need to get put on there for her breeding schedule. I lick my lips, thinking about finally fucking her without her damn birth control.

I point my finger at her to come to me as I drop my trousers on the floor. I kick my loafers off and watch as she picks up my trousers, folding them up neatly and putting them on the bed before tucking my shoes under the bed.

I go on my knees before her and peel down her lace panties to discover her cunt is covered in my cum from the load I dumped in her on the plane.

"Such a dirty slut for me. Did you like sitting all that time with my cum sticking to your cunt?"

I glance up at her, and she smiles before nodding her head. I chuckle and rub what's left of my cum over her lips and push some back inside her pussy hole. My name on her cunt is far more lasting than any marriage certificate. I finger her for a few minutes until she moans and grips my hair.

I stand up and push her back on the bed.

"Turn around I want your throat first."

She immediately rolls over and shuffles along the bed till her head is at the end of the bed. Her pink lips are wide open, and her eyes are on me. She plays with her nipples tugging at the metal piercings.

I frown at them for a moment. Shit. Will my kid be drinking from a sprinkler? I will need to ask the doctor about her nipple piercings tomorrow.

She closed her mouth and licked her lips before opening her mouth again, and my attention was back on my doll.

I grip the back of her head and place my thumbs under her jawline. I push into her hot wet mouth. She widens her mouth, and I shove my cock down her throat. She has had a year to learn how to swallow me down her neck flawlessly. The girth or the length is no longer an issue. I see her neck swell up as she continues to gobble me down.

"Such a good cocksucker, baby. You have the most perfect set of holes. My perfect, Fuckdoll," I said while filling her neck up.

I pull back and rock back and forth, surging in and out of her throat. The more saliva that gathers, the easier my motions become. I keep my eye on her, playing with her tits and the tattoo on her pussy as I fuck her throat. As soon as my balls tighten up, I ease out of her.

She whines like a needy animal. I slap her tits.

"None of that get in the bathroom. I'm going to give you what you need."

She sits up, and I help her off the bed, sending her off in the direction of the bathroom with a wallop to her ass. She wiggles her hot ass with its pink handprint and all before walking towards the bathroom.

I glance out at the beautiful view of the sea. I will need to give her a tour later. I follow her into the bathroom, and she hasn't gone in the massive bath but the specially crafted wet room I had designed. I will miss marking her with my piss. She has laid the black towel under her knees and one for her elbow, and she is bent over, waiting for me. I pause for a moment to look at her perfect set of holes.

It drives me crazy thinking about her all the time. There is no way I could ever have her living in civilisation. I would end up killing too many people or, worse hurting her.

I shake my head and get the lube, and a small butt plug out of the hidden cabinet behind the mirror. I grab a towel for myself and stalk towards my Fuckdoll.

She lifts her ass higher as I lay everything down.

"You can't wait for me to piss inside your asshole, can you? You're practically creaming yourself just kneeling here. What a dirty anal slut you are Fuckdoll," I said, knowing she loves being shamed for half the shit I do to her. "Your pussy is leaking like a damn faucet."

I lube up my dick slowly, taking my time, knowing she is horny. Living in a secluded desert with little to do but fuck was ingenious of me. She doesn't realise how primed she constantly is for me.

I squirt lube on her ass, and she parts her legs wider for me. I add some lube to my fingers, and no sooner than I've pushed them inside her, she rocks her ass back against my fingers, moaning.

Impatient now, I widen my fingers a few times before I push my thick head at her ass. Pushing till the tip slips in, I slowly keep feeding her ass until I'm deep enough to make some slow, shallow thrusts back and forth. Her ass soon loosens up, and she pushes her ass back.

I slap her ass.

"Who does the fucking?" I growl at her.

She lets out a sound between a moan and a cry and buries her face in the towel, clutching it tightly in her hands.

She wants it hard. Let me give it to her.

I rear and slammed my full length inside her, and she squeals like an animal and tries to move forward.

I grip her hips holding her ass on my dick.

"Where the fuck do you think you're going? Make up your mind, Fuckdoll," I snap at her.

I don't wait for a response, but I hold her ass as I watch my fat cock slip in and out of her hole. I'm panting within minutes.

"Rub your pussy, baby. I'm going to cum."

I grab her by her hair and hip before I fuck her loosened hole furiously, ignoring her soft cries. Each lewd sound of our flesh hitting together drove me on. I see her hand disappear between her legs and keep my thrusts hard and long. It takes her seconds to cum, and I know what she needs, so I hold myself deep and nut inside her guts.

"Take that, you filthy anal slut. Take my cum and get ready for my hot piss."

Her small back shakes as her ass tightens around my cock, causing me to suck in my breath.

Fuck Benny's plastic dolls.

My woman has the best fuck holes in the world.

CHAPTER 20

Elizabeth

His damn filthy mouth gives me the best orgasms. One time he made me cum just by playing with my nipples and using his dirty words.

I don't move my ass because I know he can't take a piss till he softens slightly. I keep rubbing my pussy because it's his problem, not mine.

When he pulls back slightly, I tense and wait for his hot stream.

"Are you ready to take my piss up your asshole, Elizabeth? Do you want me to dirty you up? My filthy little piss whore?"

I nod my head pushing back on his dick and rubbing myself harder. He groans, and I feel his hot piss jet out of his cock and begin to fill me up. I rub my clit, desperate to cum again.

"Argh, that feels so good pissing inside your asshole. My little toilet. Take it all, baby," Zak said in between breathy pants.

Between his words and his using me, my ass clamps down on him as I cum again.

"My greedy little Fuckdoll," he said with a chuckle before leaning down and playing with my tits as he continued to piss in me.

I lean my head on the towel and relax until he is finished. As soon as he pulls out of me, he puts the plug inside my asshole. He helps me up, and I groan, holding my stomach.

"You do that every time. Beg me to piss in you, then moan

and groan afterwards. You should be grateful to have my piss inside you."

I roll my eyes before he starts on a tirade that just won't stop.

"Don't be long I want to show you some of the Island before it gets dark."

I nod excitedly. How could I have forgotten we aren't in fucking Mongolia anymore?

❋ ❋ ❋

I've never appreciated such beauty in all my twenty-six years of being on this earth. Not to mention Zak is being so sweet to me that it's fucking freaking me out.

He is so proud of Esme Island. I love watching him talk about it. He has never been so animated. He holds my hand when he takes me to a stunning rose garden.

"This is where I feel closest to my mum. I've missed seeing her favourite flower," he said softly.

I look around at the flowers and surrounding grass. In this heat, the garden must have needed maintenance. I wonder if his mum has passed away.

He looks so—desolate. His head is lowered, and his massive shoulders are hunched. I pull my hand away from his and hug him. He paused for a second before he wrapped his arms around me. He buried his face into my hair and inhaled deeply.

"If I didn't want to desecrate my mother's memorial garden, I would fucking pound you into the grass right now," he whispered into my ear.

And just like that, our tender moment was ruined. I couldn't help but laugh. I've never been fucked as much in all my life as I was in Mongolia. I slap his back, and he chuckles.

"Come on, you can swim naked in the pool," he said, pulling me out of the small garden. I look back at it and know she must have been one heck of a lady for Zak to feel anything. I've not given my parents any thought at all. They were probably happy to see the back of me.

I sigh heavily and try to keep up with Zak's massive stride.

* * *

The following day I hear a boat approach the pier, and Zak comes upstairs to tell me to put some clothes on. I'm so used to wearing all the tiny pieces of clothing Zak insisted I wore in the desert. I pull on a long floral summer dress from the wardrobe. He had everything organised in the house. There was nothing that wasn't to my taste or size. I'm still trying to figure Zak out. Each time I think I have him pegged, he shifts gears.

Perhaps I never will.

I see a tall lady with brunette hair when I reach the dining room. She is laughing at something Zak is saying. The bitch is touching his arm.

I stride over to them, and Zak turns to smile at me. I ignore him and punch the bitch in the face.

"Keep your fucking hands to yourself, bitch," I snarl as she holds her cheek.

Zak has lifted me up in the air as I struggle and kick him. I aim for his balls, but my leg isn't going high enough.

"Woah. What the fuck?" he said, the shock clear in his voice.

I clamp my mouth shut. Fuck him. He let her touch him. He tossed me over his shoulder to jog upstairs and locked me in the bedroom. I throw the closest thing to me at the door sadly, it's his shoe, and it does little damage to anything.

"You fucking let her touch you, and I'm going to cut your dick off in your sleep, you asshole," I scream as loud as I can.

I look around to see if there is anything I can smash.

That fucking whoring cunt. Fucking bitch.

"Get that fucking cunt out of here," I scream again, but my

voice cracks because I've not used it for so long. So I use my fists and pound on the door.

"You're both fucking dead, Zak. Fucking both of you. You fucking bastard!"

Part of me knows I'm acting insane the other part is livid.

He made me into this. I put my back on the door and slide down it till my ass hits the floor. Tears pour out of my eyes and roll down my face.

What am I without Zak?

Who am I?

Sobs rack through my body now uncontrollably. I sink my head onto my knees, not wanting to know the answer to any of my questions.

CHAPTER 21

Zak

I've not been caught off guard for years. That definitely did. I listen to the profanities coming out of Elizabeth's mouth in shock. Hearing her pound on the door like a crazy woman, but it was her soft cries before she broke into full-on sobbing that almost made me open the door.

I'm torn between trying to pacify her or leaving to get rid of the fucking Doctor. I need to process this turn of events.

I run downstairs, and the woman is holding her cheek. I almost roll my eyes. What a pussy. I waited to hear what she had to say first, so I knew what action to take. The last thing I need is any legal issues. I stand there staring at her till she cracks.

"Why did she just go crazy and punch me like that?"

I narrow my eyes on her. If anyone is going to berate my doll, it's fucking me.

"Watch your mother fucking tone. That's my wife. She wouldn't have punched you if you hadn't put your paws on me. Is this what sort of a professional you are?"

I know as soon as she has a guilty look on her face. What I took for friendliness, Elizabeth saw it for what it was.

"Have you seen how stunning my wife is? You think I would ever look at anyone else?"

She puts her hand away from her jaw and straightens her back. Before she gives me any of her bullshit and I bury the cunt on my Island. I nip it in the bud.

"Do you want me to report you to the medical board for inappropriate behaviour?"

She purses her lips and shakes her head.

"Good. Now get the fuck off my Island. If you ever even think about my wife, I will fucking hunt you down and make sure I ruin your life. You know I have the means to do so."

I watch her pick up her bag and leave my home. The bitch left a bad taste in my mouth. No wonder I hate people.

I wince, thinking about Elizabeth. Other than our one spat, she had been perfectly well-behaved.

I would have done worse had the roles been reversed. I would have slit the man's throat and fucked Elizabeth in his pool of blood.

I walked outside to see if the bitch had left my Island. I want peace and harmony on my Island. My eye catches my mother's garden, and I decide to go and sit with her for a while. It didn't feel the same in Mongolia without her flowers being there. My eyes focus on the beach and the surrounding beauty of the Island.

What do I do with my Fuckdoll now?

* * *

When I unlocked the door to the bedroom, I poked my head in first in case she decided to bash my head in after she had cried herself out. My heart softens slightly more when I see her lying curled up on the bed with her back towards the door.

I walk across the room and toe my shoes off and cautiously move onto the bed closer to her.

"Did you fuck her?" She asked in a monotone voice. "Was she better than me?" She said with a sniffle.

Usually, emotions and crying have little to no effect on me, but I know what she is feeling.

I pull her towards me, ignoring her, trying to claw the edge of the bed to pull herself away from me as if her puny ass is any match against my size or strength.

I choose my words carefully because this will be the only time I will explain myself to her.

"When I was around four or five, my father was beating me, and my mum pushed me in a cupboard under the stairs, and my father beat the fuck out of her. I stayed under the stairs and fell asleep. My mum came and took me. We left the house in the middle of the night."

She turns to face me, and my pretty doll's eyes are swollen and red. She still has tears running down her eyes. I use my thumbs and wipe them away before kissing her forehead. When she places her hand on my chest, I pull her close and tuck her head under my chin.

"Do you know the statistics of men and women who stay with abusive partners?"

I feel her shake her head.

"Let's put it this way, the majority never leave, or if they do, the damage done remains with you for life. My mother was brave enough to leave him for me."

I stroke the soft strands of blonde hair until my hand reaches the base of her head, and I leave my hand resting on the nape of her neck.

"We lived in a homeless centre for a while. It was scary as a kid. There were so many alcoholics and junkies there. Eventually, the council gave us a small shitty apartment in the city. My mum could have lived from the government benefits and had an easier life, but she told me she never wanted me to grow up on handouts and not have aspirations. It's why I was at the charity foundation that night."

Her head shoots up, and her eyes are wide with regret.

"I'm sorry, Zak. I was such an asshole back then," she said grimly.

I smile at her and shake my head. She doesn't want to know my sick thoughts of why I took her *because* of that night.

"Mum worked when I was in school, and then she would work nights cleaning in a second job. The flat wasn't pleasant, it had bad mould in it. As she got older, her health declined. I went to university determined to make something of myself to look after my mother. My brain was going all over the place trying to invent the next big application when they were just getting up and running. Long story short, I was working day and night. I spoke to my mother often, but she never told me she had cancer. I carried on working. I was on top of the world. My best friend was helping me with the app, I had a girlfriend, and my mother's life was about to get easier."

I take a long heavy breath before exhaling it slowly.

"I had no idea my mum was ill. When I spoke to the doctors, they told me it was an aggressive cancer, and they had given her weeks to live, but she had survived for months. My mother's encouragement drove me forward. She hung on for me. I came home three days too late."

I clear my throat before I continue.

"Mum died, and Jessica was fucking my best friend. I just moved on to destroying lives, working my ass off to be successful. Then I saw you at the foundation event, and my friend Benny said something, and I took you."

It wasn't my place to tell Elizabeth about Benny's harem.

"Do you think after someone cheated on me and I never fucked another woman for nine whole years before I met you, that I would fuck some nasty bitch over my perfect doll?" I said to her softly.

She looks up at me again but gives me a watery smile this time.

"My mother was everything to me, she was the one person I knew loved me more than life itself. By losing her, I lost a large part of myself. It made me think I was as dark as my father. It's why I stay away from people. I have no patience for humans. The majority of them are cunts," I said, pausing to think about getting that implant out of her arm. "And now I need to get you a new doctor."

Her head snaps up.

"I don't want a female doctor."

I narrow my eyes at her. "I don't want another man touching you," I snap at her sharply.

She frowns at me.

"What about someone in their 70s?" She asked.

I sigh.

"What about an old lady doctor?"

"No, she will still want to feel you up like that fucking nasty bitch."

"I won't have another man touching you. It will never happen —"

I paused after I had another thought.

"Unless it's our son."

I wrap my arms around her, remembering what I said to the doctor.

"I want us to get married. If anyone does or says anything after they see our rings, we can murder them chop them up and piss on their bones before we bury them on our Island," I said, curious to see what she would say.

She lets out a small laugh.

"Sure, bring that cunt back, and I will happily do it."

Fuck, yeah. She is the one for me.

"Now, about you breaking my rules—"

CHAPTER 22

Elizabeth

He has gagged me and left me lying on the bed. For two days, he has fucked my ass non-stop. I have no idea why he thinks that it's punishment at this point. Perhaps he is getting it out of his system because I am getting the implant out today.

In the end, he found a lesbian nurse in her 50s, and he wasn't happy about that in case she hit on me. He wouldn't tell me how he knew about her sexual orientation, either.

He comes into the bedroom, his face like thunder. He unties my wrists and takes the gag out of my mouth. I rotate my jaw. He put the largest one in because of the amount I swore.

He stomps into the walk-in closet and has his clothes in his hand. He throws one of his black T-shirts with his three-quarter-length bottoms at me.

"No, wait. Let me get you a bra. Wear a fucking bra."

I ignore him and shove his bottoms on and check the length. They reach my ankles. He throws a bra at my head. I quickly put it on since he seems to be at boiling point. He walks over and shoves the T-shirt over my head.

We go downstairs and into the living room. The nurse stands up and smiles widely at us.

"Mrs Henderson. It's lovely to meet you. My name is Josie. Your husband said you are both ready for a family. This is wonderful news. I brought some information for you that you might find useful."

I tighten my hand in Zak's hand.

"Hi, Josie. Thank you, that would be great. If we can just remove this implant, that's all we need today."

I need this done and her out of here. Zak is as stiff as a board.

"Yes, of course. It won't take long at all."

✻ ✻ ✻

I wonder how hard I want to be fucked to get pregnant. I sit at the dresser rubbing moisturiser on my face while Zak lies on the bed with his nose in a book.

"Josie was nice," I said casually.

His head snapped up instantly, and he lowered the book on his chest.

"What the fuck do you mean by that?"

I bite the inside of my lip to keep a straight face.

"She was friendly and left us all that extra information."

He glares at me briefly before his face relaxes. "You wouldn't last an hour with her. She doesn't have a cock, and I know how hungry you get for my cock, Fuckdoll."

"There are always double-ended dildos," I said with a snigger.

His eyes darken, and he throws his book on the floor. I sense the danger and dash towards the bathroom.

He dives off the bed and reaches me in a few quick strides.

"Oh, we are done in the bathroom for a long time. Double-ended dick? By the time I am done with you, your pussy will be in too much pain for you to think about a lesbian with a plastic cock."

He picks me up and throws me over his shoulder, knocking my breath out.

I'm definitely getting fucked so hard tonight.

Five days later, I lie on the bed with an ice pack on my pussy. I won't be teasing him like that again.

He strolls in, carrying our breakfast on a tray.

"How's my pussy doing?" He asked in a smug voice.

I glare at him.

"I am going to be limping up the aisle with a broken pussy."

He chuckles.

"You know you won't need to walk anywhere."

That's true. Benny is going to officiate our marriage online. He has been running Zak's company. I didn't know it then, but Zak had a satellite phone and internet connection, and he kept in touch with Benny and an eye on my missing person's case.

We are on a remote Island in Thailand I doubt anyone would ever recognise me, let alone report seeing me on Esme Island. Zak is very selective about whom he allows access to the island.

* * *

We sit out in his mother's garden with the laptop set up on a table. We sit on the bench. Zak has me sitting on his lap.

Benny's call comes through.

"It's about time. We were about to get a professional officiant who knows how to tell the time," Zak snarks at Benny.

Benny is wearing a priest's collar and shirt.

"I had to get ready and look the part. Anyway, I have officiated three weddings. You think I live with my wives in sin?"

"He has three wives?" I whispered to Zak. Confused by how many wives Benny had.

"I will tell you later," he whispers back.

"Dearly beloved, we are gathered here today to join—"

"This isn't what we agreed to, Benny," Zak interrupts.

"I know, I'm fucking with you."

I peer at the laptop screen and see three women behind Benny sitting there.

When Benny sees me looking, he rolls his chair away and introduces me to his three wives. My eyes widen, and I remember what Zak told me about seeing me at the foundation and his conversation with Benny.

I want to laugh so badly, but I don't want to offend Benny—or his doll wives.

It all makes sense now. I turn around to Zak and kiss him. I hold his face in my hands after he stops devouring my lips.

"I love you so much, Zak Henderson."

"Hey. Hey, guys. I haven't even started yet," Benny protests.

Zak's eyes darken, and I can see their tumultuous emotions. I drop a kiss on his lips.

"You don't need to say anything. I just wanted you to know," I told him.

His face relaxes, and he kisses me again slowly. This time we both ignore Benny's protests.

CHAPTER 23

Zak

I carry my wife through the house and upstairs. It doesn't matter what title she has. She will always be my Fuckdoll.

Fucking, Benny, dressing his dolls up and sitting them in the background. I should be grateful he put clothes on them. He was doing an amazing job with our company. If not for that fact, I would doubt his mental faculties.

Elizabeth's declaration surprised me, and tonight I am going to make sweet love to my wife.

She has her arm wrapped around my neck and is playing with the back of my hair. My mind goes to when she punched the doctor in her face. We will either make crazy children, or we might get lucky.

We reach our bedroom, and I lay her on the bed. She is wearing a short white lace dress with half sleeves. I didn't want Benny perving on her. I watched him interact with her, and I got no bad signals.

"Are you ready to get your eggs fertilised?"

"Isn't that what you've been doing for the past five days," she asked with her voice as dry as the Gobi desert.

"I'm letting your sass go only because it's our wedding day," I said, running my hands up my doll's bare legs.

She is beginning to tan, and her skin looks as if it is glowing. We have the freedom of the Island, and I love keeping her naked.

She sits up and struggles to reach her zip behind her. I kneel over her legs and push her hands away to find the tiny zip is undone by a few inches, but it's caught in the material.

I grip the material with both hands and rip it off her. I expected her to complain, but when I looked at her, her big blue eyes were full of desire. She lowers her gaze down my neck, and she unbuttons my shirt.

Once she tugs my shirt off, she kisses my chest before pulling my neck down she licks my beard near my ear.

"I'm so wet for you right now. I want you to fuck me like a sex doll, use my holes and cum in them. I want to wear your cum all over my body like your personal little fuck doll," she whispers sexily in my ear before licking it, and her roving hands pinch my nipples.

I gulp hard as images fly through my head at the speed of light. Unfortunately, I will be unable to make sweet love to my wife tonight.

I fly off the bed, rip my trousers off, gather everything I need, and bring it back to dump some on the bed and some on the side table.

"Get off the bed and take your dress off," I said harshly.

I ripped the back open, but she was still wearing it.

"You want to be my set of holes for me to use?" I asked her as I watched her slide her dress off.

She is wearing a sheer white bra that covers nothing. When my eyes drop to her pussy, I understand what's got her cunt so hot.

Beneath a scrap of lace, a set of pearls sat perfectly in her pussy.

"Turn around and bend over. Hold your ankles."

The white pearls run along her asshole and dip into her pussy," I said, walking closer.

"Sit on the bed and show me your cunt."

Once she is on the bed and opens her legs, and beside my name is a set of pearls inside her cunt.

"When did you get these?"

"I ordered them for tonight. They came a few days ago."

Her pussy lips are glistening from her arousal, and those pearls have been inside her slit, rubbing her while we were getting married. I slowly look over her body till I reach her face.

She has just unleashed a beast.

"You want to be my doll? I can use you anywhere at anytime? You swallow down anything I offer you?"

She licks her lips as if she is tasting me and nods her head.

Dark and depraved thoughts fill my mind, and I walk into the bathroom and bring a stack of towels back. I lay several of them on the floor.

"Get on your knees. Keep your legs wide open. I want to see your cunt at all times."

I grip my cock, watching her kneel beside the bed.

"Open your cock sucking mouth."

She sits with her pussy on show and her mouth wide open. She has tilted her head back, ready to take whatever I want to give her. My dick has never felt harder, and my balls are already tightening.

"My pretty wife is such a cock hungry whore. Hungry for my cum and thirsty for my piss."

Moving closer to her, I sit my balls on her face rubbing them all over her before sitting them in her mouth. I don't need to say anything. My perfect doll begins to suckle them one by one before licking them. I pull back because my pre-cum is about to start leaking out of my dick.

I drip it over her face, wanking out more to rub it over her lips.

"When I watched them work on your lips, this is all I could think of. These perfect lips were ready for me. Ready to swallow all of me down."

I ignore my cock as it jerks. I watch a long strand of pre-cum drip inside her mouth. It disappears down her throat. I place the tip of my cock on her tongue and rub myself as more trickles on her tongue.

"Taste me, my little hungry whore. Then lick me clean, don't waste a single drop."

I watch her swallow before she licks the thick head of my cock. Her little tongue dug into my cock hole. I dig my fingers into my cock and wank some more for her. She wraps her lips around my head and sucks my cock, and drinks me down. Her tongue flicks over my cock slit repeatedly until I'm breathing as if I've been running.

"You need more, don't you? My greedy little Fuckdoll."

Her blue eyes move to mine, and she nods her head. I smile at her.

I've got so much more for her.

I push my dick inside her mouth, and when I come across the tight opening at the back of her throat, I hold her head and thrust hard, forcing myself down her throat.

She moans through it. She woke up the beast in me and will now pay the price.

I lean back to her and see she has swallowed around six inches of me. I move back slightly and fuck my whole cock down her throat, and after the initial thrust, I feel her swallowing, and she wraps her lips around the base.

"Suck a good cock sucker, baby. You should sleep with my dick in your mouth tonight. I can wake up in the morning to cum and piss inside that filthy mouth."

She moved her tongue around the base of my cock, making me need to fuck her.

I hold her head with both hands and thrust in and out of her mouth, moving my ass fast and hard. I ignore the gurgling and choking sounds she makes. I watch her tears fall from her eyes and join her messy face.

"Such a good fuck hole," I growl out. "You want my cum? Do you want to taste my cum? Wear it proudly?"

Her eyes move to mine, and she nods.

"Let me use your fuckhole first, make it nice and sore so you can remember me using your mouth hole tomorrow," I said, breathing heavily.

Her hand goes between her legs, and she rubs her pussy.

I slow down because I want to feel every crevice in her mouth and neck. It's not long before I resume fucking her hard and fast again.

I pulled out when I felt my orgasm approach.

"Keep that fuck hole open for me," I said, yanking her hair backwards so her hole was flat and facing the ceiling.

I only needed to tug my cock twice, and my cum spurted out.

"Drink it, Fuckdoll. Savour my cum in your mouth."

Thick cum keeps pouring out of me I can't stop the groans and sounds of relief as I watch my beautiful wife take my cum in her mouth. I lift my dick and squeeze the few droplets out. I wipe it off with my thumb and stick it in her mouth.

"Drink it all down and suck me clean."

She swallows several times before she licks my thumb.

I laughed, as it was a lot of cum. I pull my thumb out and place my dick on her face, rubbing it over her eyes, nose, and both sides of her cheek.

"My filthy, Fuckdoll."

She takes the tip of my dick and swirls her tongue around it before sucking me by moving her head back and forth over the tip while she holds my dick in her mouth. I know what she needs.

"Do you want more, Fuckdoll?" I asked in a husky voice, and my dick twitched in her mouth at the thought of her taking everything.

She nods her head before continuing to suck me off.

I've never been more grateful for choosing her to become my perfect doll because that's what she is, fucking perfection.

I pull out of her mouth and reach behind her to unhook her bra. She eagerly takes it off, making me smile.

113

"Open your hole for me."

She opens her mouth, I push my dick inside her throat again, and she wraps her lips around me. I focus and try to ignore my semi-hard dick and exhale a long puff of breath as I feel my piss stream down her neck.

"Ugh. Yeah, drink it down, my dirty whore."

I glance down at her closed eyes as she drinks my hot piss. I slide my cock out of her throat and watch her mouth fill up. She gasps, and it runs down her mouth. I pull out and piss on her tits. She leans back and sticks her tits out for me.

I know I'm almost done, so I point down at her pussy and watch as my piss splashes over her tiny panties and my tattoo.

As soon as I'm done. I wipe any excess off me and throw some towels on the bed. I wipe her down and toss her onto the bed.

I kneel down and spread her thighs to devour my wife's filthy cunt.

I push the pearls to one side and start on her clit. Sucking, licking and flicking my tongue on her.

She is crying, moaning and writhing on the bed. I ignore everything. I lift her ass and lick down her slit, using my tongue to push the pearls into her cunt. I have got to look up some pearl accessories for her. Her cunt has never looked prettier.

I grab her hips and turn her over. I continue to lick along the pearls till I reach her puckered little asshole.

"Is this hole hungry too? My dirty anal slut."

I lick around the pearls before licking her asshole. I push my tongue inside her. It doesn't take long for my tongue to slip inside her ass. I fuck her asshole with my tongue for a few moments till she shudders on the bed.

I pull off her and put my hand on her back.

"You only cum on my cock, Fuckdoll. You'll lick my cum clean off my fingers after I nut in your holes."

She is never going to leave this Island. She is never going to leave me.

CHAPTER 24

Elizabeth

I 've never been happier than in this moment, and it's not because Zak has his tongue in my ass. Okay, it's partly because of that.

We got married. It was perfect, and I'm going to cum so hard because the stupid panties edged me for fucking hours.

I feel him pull away from me, and I groan in protest into the bed. His hand covers my lower back.

"You only cum on my cock, Fuckdoll. You'll lick my cum clean off my fingers after I nut in your holes," he said in a dark and ominous voice.

I don't need to turn to look at him to know he is wearing his murderous expression.

Oh, yes. Please.

When he slaps my ass hard, I raise it higher for more. I hear his sharp intake of breath before he rips my panties off. The tiny balls of torment scatter and fall on the floor.

"I don't love you, Elizabeth," he growls out.

A fiery slice of pain stabs my chest, and I feel sick as his harsh words sink in.

"Love doesn't describe what I feel for you. You fucking leached yourself into my damn soul. That. Was. Never. Supposed. To happen," he said, but his final words were bellowed at me with accompanying vicious slaps on my ass.

My eyes well up, and I look over my shoulder and see the

turmoil on his face. I tell him the only thing that I know will make us complete.

"Give me your seed, Zak," I said in a firm voice.

He blinks at me momentarily before I see the pain and rage slip away from his face. A ghost of a smile plays on his lips, and his face morphs into mischievousness. He drops onto my back, knocking the wind out of me, but he quickly lifts one hand on the bed, and the other reaches to push his cock inside me.

He doesn't hesitate to slam his dick inside me. I cry out as he hits deep inside of me. The man doesn't stop there, he fucks in and out of me furiously, smacking into my ass with each deep thrust. I can't move or breathe properly at the speed of his hard strokes. He yanks my head up, gripping my hair painfully.

"You want me to breed your cunt?"

How is he not out of breath?

I nod my head ignoring the searing pain in my scalp. He lets go of my hair, and I feel his hands reach my breasts. He grips them in his palms, holds me upright, and piles drive into me.

He pauses to grind in and out of me, rubbing me deep inside, and I moan and push my ass against him. I reach for my clit, desperate to come while he ruins me.

As soon as I tighten around him, he resumes hammering in and out of me. The only sounds in the room are our grunting breaths and flesh slapping together. When he pinches my nipples between his thumb and fingers, I begin to shake. I close my eyes and lean back against him as the waves of sheer ecstasy rip through me. I feel a gush of liquid pour out of me as I clench down on his thick cock. I cry out my relief, and I feel my body relax. He releases one breast and puts his hand on my belly, and pushes himself deeper inside me.

He grunts, and I feel him shoot his cum inside me. I remember his taste on my tongue and lips, and my pussy contracts around him again. He moans, and his hands grip my breast and belly so tight I know he will leave bruises behind. We collapse on the bed and pant like distressed animals.

I smile on the bed. I'm so glad he had the hindsight to put

towels on the bed. I cannot physically move right now.

He rolls us to our side, but he leaves his cock buried inside me. We lay there in comfortable silence for a while. His hand moved over my head and body as if he couldn't get enough of touching me. When he pulls away from me, I moan. He slaps my hip.

"I'm going to fill the bath up before you start bitching about your pussy being sore again."

I stretch my aching body on the bed. It will be a long night, and I can't wait.

❊ ❊ ❊

It was six weeks later, we found out I was pregnant. It took me a long time to believe it was true. I insisted on taking four different brands of pregnancy testing kits before I believed a baby was growing inside of me. It was weird to have Zak watching me pee for a change.

Since our wedding night, I have accepted that Zak will never stray from me. His obsession with me is beyond my comprehension. I'm jealous, but I'm not crazy. In the end, I agreed to an older female doctor because he promised me he would kill her if she hit on him.

See, I'm completely sane.

CHAPTER 25

Zak

D o I deserve my pretty doll? Probably not, but since she is mine now, she will never leave my sight for as long as she lives and breathes.

I glance down at the four tests she insisted on and pick them up from the bathroom bin. I open up my black lockbox and put them in there.

The box contained hundreds of photos of Elizabeth when I followed her for nine months. The only other pictures in there are the three men whom I butchered when they couldn't take the hint to leave her alone. Their faces have been scratched out in the pictures. My eye twitches in anger when I think about them. I should have taken longer to kill them.

I lay the pregnancy tests neatly before closing the lid and locking it. I take the box into our closet and open up the secret panel. I slide the box alongside my mother's box and lock it up before sliding the panel back over it.

Satisfaction courses through me when I stand up.

Everything is in order.

I go down to the pool, where my pregnant doll awaits me.

❊ ❊ ❊

Six weeks later, when my Fuckdoll walks out of the bathroom and approaches the bed, I sit up.

"What the fuck?" I gasped out in surprise.

She starts crying at my words, and I regret my harsh tone.

"I'm not going to be perfect anymore or pretty. I'm going to be the size of an elephant," She wails before moving to the side to show me her protruding belly.

As soon as I see the swell of her belly sticking out at the side, my dick hardens. That's a part of me she has inside of her. My mouth dries out as I glance further up and see her tits look bigger and heavier. There is no way her stomach was that big yesterday.

"Come here, Fuckdoll," I said with my voice so hoarse my words came out in a croak.

I whip the covers back and rub my dick.

"I don't give a fuck if you get to the size of a whale. You're carrying my seed inside you, so stop your crying and get over here, now," I snap at her.

I reach into the bedside drawer and get the vibrator and lube out.

She is still standing in front of the bed but looking at me in shock.

"Get on the bed, flat on your back. Move it."

I smirk when that gets her moving. Fucking crying over stupid shit. She is lucky she is pregnant.

"If you ever think I won't want you or think you are anything but my perfect pretty doll. I will get the giant plug and leave it inside you for a whole fucking week," I growl at her watching her lie on the bed.

I climb out of bed and walk around to face her crazy hormonal ass.

I take in her face, her swollen tits and her bulging belly before my eyes reach my name scrawled over her. My dick leaks over the floor.

119

"Does this look like I give a damn?" I growl at her as I grab my aching cock.

She lowers her head to look at my rock-hard dick. Her tears are gone, and she smiles and shakes her head.

"Bad, Fuckdoll. You should know better," I said in a calmer voice.

I lube up the small vibrator and push it slowly into her asshole. I drop down to my knees and watch her hole stretch out before I slide it in and out of her hole. I wish I could fuck her asshole like I used to, but I have read up on everything I can and can't do to her holes while she is pregnant. I exhale heavily. I can wait until she has the baby and heals before ravaging her again.

I switch the vibrator on and leave it inside her. Standing up, I lean over her and suck her soft pink nipples. They definitely look bigger. My cock rubs on her swollen belly and leaks all over her. I rub against it harder.

"As soon as your body is ready, I will fuck you so hard that you never forget what you are to me. My. Fucking. Fuckdoll."

I squeeze her tits together and suck everything in my mouth. Her nipples and barbells. I suck and lick them until she squirms beneath me, moaning and gripping at my hair painfully.

I slide down lower and kiss her belly. I rub my lips on my pool of pre-cum before I raise my lips to hers.

"Lick my lips, taste how much I need you," I whispered to her.

She raises her head and licks my lips before closing her eyes and moans.

"My greedy, Fuckdoll," I said with a chuckle.

I kiss her rosy lips, push her mouth open with my tongue, gather my saliva in my mouth, and drip it into her mouth. Before I push my tongue inside her mouth, rubbing and sliding mine against hers.

I rub my dick against her pussy to find her drenched. I stand up and push her legs over my arms stretching her wide open for me to fuck into her cunt without touching her belly. This way, I can see everything. My dick twitches inside her hole. I glance down and push the tip further inside I feel the slight vibrations in her ass.

"Play with your cunt. I am going to nut so fast inside your tight hole," I said through clenched teeth.

I watch her small hand slide down her belly and rub her clit. Satisfied that her holes are sufficiently stuffed. I push her legs open wider and hold them apart before I push inside her watching my dick disappear into her pussy to the root. I grip her tight and thrust into her hard and fast. The vibrations run along my dick each time I slam inside her.

She grinds herself on me, but I don't stop moving back and forth in the most perfect pussy hole ever created. It's not long before I hammer away inside her, with her leaking all down my balls. I glance up at her to see her eyes are closed her pussy tightens around me. Her tits are bouncing up and down with each one of my thrusts.

I close my eyes as I feel my balls rear up, and I roar out her name as my orgasm hits a crescendo. The sight, the smell, and the sounds all merge into one. Her gush of cum on my dick sucks me in deeper, and I groan as my cock continues to spurt out jets of cum inside her. I pull back slightly, rubbing the head of my cock back and forth, prolonging my pleasure as her cunt flutters around me.

When I've unloaded myself, I pull out and watch my cum pour out of her pussy and drip down her holes in triumph.

Size of an elephant, my ass.

CHAPTER 26

Elizabeth

I squeeze Zak's hand so tightly that he pulls his hand away to push his fingers between mine, and he squeezes my hand in reassurance. He glances away from me again, returning to the small black screen.

I was ready for one baby, but two?

Am I truly surprised? I wouldn't put it past him to have stored all his cum from his nine-year celibacy period, and he inserted it inside me every night with a turkey baster. I let out a snigger at the thought.

He looks back at me sharply, his eyes suspicious, but he returns his attention back to the screen.

Sheesh, it's as if he has the hormonal imbalance.

We listen on as the doctor leaves us with information on multiple pregnancies. I grimace at the thought of Zak scrutinising everything and all the extra restrictions he will put on me.

He has turned one of the spare rooms into a medical centre. I'm sure we have more equipment than a clinic at this point.

As soon as Zak dismisses the doctor. Who is old and has never once touched Zak. He scanned me from top to bottom before a smug, self-satisfied grin spread across his face.

And so it begins.

❊ ❊ ❊

I never heard the end of it about his super sperm. If I didn't love him and our babies so much, I would have stabbed him in the face by now. The man loved me, cared for me, rubbed my swollen ankles and feet, cooked for me, and talked to the twins as if they were already here. I never thought he would be as excited as me to meet them.

I will never be able to understand this extraordinary man.

On the flip side, he drove me insane by never leaving my side and bitching about everything. Walking downstairs alone, my bath water being too hot, not drinking enough water. The worst of it was the vanilla sex. It didn't matter how much I tried to piss him off until he fucked me hard. Nothing worked.

The only thing that gave me hope was that he told me he had made a list of everything I had done and said to him that broke our rules, and I would be paying for each infraction for a very long time.

For the most part, I can't ever remember being this happy. I cringe thinking of the man I would have ended up with. It would have been someone as stuffy as my father. I feel a little sick come up in my mouth thinking about it.

"I told you to walk a little after eating. I read up—"

"Yes, dear," I said, interrupting him, but he continued.

I close my eyes and ignore him, he goes into his tirades like a little bitch at times. I smile, thinking about our time in Mongolia and wonder if the cabin is still there.

I open one eye to look at him.

He is still going on about my insides being squashed up and how exercise is supposed to help my digestion.

"Ugh, my breasts hurt so much."

He stops talking and looks down at my bulging boobs straining from the bikini top.

He took the barbells out, but he will get his balls snipped after the twins. As much as we love our children, we both miss our usual activities. He had become anxious about the labour.

I keep an innocent look on my face when he moves over to my lounger and unties my bikini. All his focus is on my breasts as he bares them.

I take my breasts and squeeze them together. He groans and buries his face in my breasts.

Do I play up, claiming it's hormones, and I'm horny?

Sure, but it stops his lectures.

EPILOGUE

Elizabeth

The following Halloween

I am going to die at the cuteness overload as I place I fix my babies' cushions around them for the perfect holiday pictures.

Esme and Easton are almost three months old, and I may have sneakily ordered matching pumpkin rompers with tiny pumpkin hats. We made some beautiful babies. I might need Zak to undo his vasectomy.

I stand back, pleased that the scene is complete with cobwebs, spiders, stuffed monster animals and a black cat.

I take all the pictures very quickly, to my heart's content. Why Zak hates Halloween so much is beyond my understanding. He said the only thing he loves about it is the fact that he took me that night. Technically, it was the morning after Halloween, but he glared at me when I told him that.

"No. What have you done to my children?" Zak's voice moans from behind me.

"What? They look adorable," I replied shamelessly.

His hands travel from my waist to under my vest to squeeze my breasts. I feel my vest soak through as he massages my breasts. His fingers pinch my nipples, forcing more milk out. I feel his dick rub my ass.

"Have they fed yet?" His voice was husky with need.

I clench my thighs together.
I love this filthy man beyond words.

Zak

Six years later

I watch Esme and Easton play in the massive play area we built next to my mother's garden. I had wanted them close to the woman who would have loved them as much as I do.

My children will never need to worry about what I did as a child. They have had a home surrounded by love, not poverty and strife.

Their mother was determined they never take anything for granted as she grew up spoilt. Somehow between the two of us, we found the perfect balance.

My children have my dark hair, but they have their mother's lighter eyes. If they have my deviousness, it hasn't shown yet, but I look out for it and would welcome it. I would never make them feel different. They would embrace who they are.

Our home has so much love that sometimes it's too much for me to process. Some days I wake up in a cold sweat, thinking I am back in my cold and lonely mansion in England. It took one thought to change my world. Benny's plastic dolls. Thankfully, he has a real woman now. We share the work and the rewards. If anyone deserved to become my partner, it was him.

I watch Elizabeth leave the house with a tray of drinks and snacks. She still looks like my pretty Fuckdoll, and that will never change.

Nothing from the outside world touches my family. They have the best education, healthcare and a loving home on an Island paradise. My wife will never need anything but me.

I smile, hearing my children giggle.

It's one of the most beautiful sounds in my world. The other one is the sounds that come out of my wife.

She approaches us with a big smile on her perfectly painted lips.

My pretty doll.

The End.

AFTERWORD

Hello Lovelies,

Please do not even ask me how this book came about because I have no clue. It's another one that wasn't planned that snuck into my head & refused to leave. These two definitely took me by surprise. Zak was utterly depraved and twisted in every way possible.

I hope you enjoyed their crazy, twisted story & let me know if you want more like it because I had so much fun writing this one. I did question my sanity a few times, but luckily it passed.

As always and forever, thank you for your support & kind words. You **ALL** drive me forward.

Stay Happy & Stay Healthy.

With all my Love,

LoveBite Shorts xXx

BOOKS BY THIS AUTHOR

Aaron's Pet (The Pet Play Series Book 1)

Aaron Lewis billionaire businessman sees Willow and decides he wants her. When she not only refuses but insults him he is furious. He lays out a trap forcing her to bend to his will. Five months of Willow being my little pet bitch will teach her the lesson she needs.

Willow Parker a barista in the city. It's a menial job but it pays the bills. When she is propositioned by Aaron's staff member she is furious and rejects his offer of money and an illicit liaison. Now he is not only threatening her but with what she holds most dear to her heart. She just needs to survive five months with him...

The Bullied Omega: Rejected Mate ~ Reverse Harem

Warning: Initial Non-consensual heat/rut, bullying,

Alpha triplets, reverse harem, pregnancy, rejected mate, other woman drama & multiple POVs.

Cedar and her Omega mother live in the Creekwood pack. They are given a shack to live in on the boundary of their property. Cedar is lost when her mother dies. Left alone yet surrounded by pack members…who despise her. When an incident occurs Cedar is left with no alternative but to fight against the very nature of her dynamic.

This is a story of her journey from being the bullied Omega of the pack to becoming much more…

Cedar's story is not for the faint hearted.

Devilish Demon (The Monster Series Book 1)

Dubious Consent, breeding, manipulation and humiliation. Will contain a small element of MFM as well as initial NonCon.

Please Do Not Purchase if you are a sensitive reader.

Asmodeus is one of the Princes of Hell. He has had many names over the years. One is always recurring. The Prince of Lust. When one of his minions finally find the descendant of the duo who helped bind and banish him. He needs his revenge. Leaving the pits of Hell to find her. She's going to be dragged down into Hell. He will degrade her in every way possible. For hundreds of years, he has waited for his revenge. He will ensure she bears his demon spawn. Tainting any future lineage.

Claudia inherits a house from a distant relative that she never knew had existed. Deserted at a church doorstep as a baby. She finally has some information about her roots. A handsome stranger appears at the property offering his help. In exchange, she must agree to a pact with him…

Breeding Her ~ The Dark Edition: The Complete Collection ~ Books 1 To 4 (Breeding Her - The Dark Edition)

Breeding Her - The Dark Edition - Books 1-4

In British English some spelling will differ to USA

Some or all books include blackmail, dubious consent, profanity, violence, manipulation, breeding and stalking. Small element of cheating in Book 1.

If you are a sensitive reader, please Do Not Purchase.

There are no Hero's here.

There will always be some form of a HEA. The

journey our ladies face will not be an easy one it will be very LONG and HARD indeed.

Breeding His Wife - Arranged Marriage - Book One

Stefano Di Caprio has just become Capo of New York. His deceased, father had arranged a marriage for him. He intends to use this marriage for his gain, his legacy. She will conform or she will face the beast.

Caterina Abella is a carefree dreamer. Her Papa has put off her dream for years. Never divulging to her that her life is not her own to live, nor does she have the right to dream. Now she has 3 days to marry a cruel man who has very little regard for any woman. The only language he knows is violence.

Seeding Her Flower - Obsessive Stalker Book Two

Adrian Hawthorn a Tech Mughal Genius has an orderly life. Everything in its place. A routine for every aspect of his life. Until one day his existence is thrown into chaos. He sees a bright light inside Leilani so he does what any normal person would do, he follows her home…

Leilani is determined to bring her grandmother's florist shop out of the dark ages. She is approached by Adrian Hawthorn a website designer. Is his proposition too good to be true?

Breeding Her On Holiday - Held Captive Book Three

Sara has actually won something for the first time in her life. A holiday to a private Island. She was bringing a friend, but she got hurt in a freak accident. She decides to be brave and go alone. She did not get the welcome she was expecting...

Daniel seen Sara. He is keeping her. Alone on his private Island with nowhere to run. He is going to make sure he breeds her every day and night till she gives him what he wants. Everything.

Breeding His Personal Assistant - Blackmailed - Book Four

Torian

She walks around the office as if she is a ray of sunshine. Smiling at everyone. Swaying her backside in her tight little skirts. Wearing her little camisole tops or see-through blouses. A man can only take so much. It's time to make her submit to her CEO.

Riah

My boss is so grumpy. No matter how much I smile or try and make him smile. He is always picking faults in my clothes or my work. I need this job, or I would tell him where to go. What I didn't expect was for him to bend me over his desk and tell me he was going to take everything that I've been flaunting to him. The CEO has finally lost the plot.

Printed in Great Britain
by Amazon

29725753R00081